MEET

Fortune of the Month: Steven Fortune

Age: 32

Vital Statistics: ... permanent spa... could make a g... mention that he...

Claim to Fame: ...endian Fortune has been building up Rambling Rose one construction project at a time.

Romantic Prospects: Steven has looks, skills, charm and money. He's used to being catered to, flirted with and pursued by attractive women. What he's not used to is being challenged. But... he kind of likes it.

"I'll admit it—I'm having a little bit of trouble staying focused when Ellie Hernandez is around. The mayor of Rambling Rose is like no one I have ever met. She's not impressed by my family name or my wealth. But I can tell she likes me. I like her, too...more than I should.

"Under the circumstances, however, a conventional relationship is out of the question. Did I mention that Ellie is pregnant? My brothers think I was crazy to propose to her. Maybe I was. But she understands that this is a temporary fix. We both know love doesn't last..."

THE FORTUNES OF TEXAS:
Rambling Rose

Dear Reader,

I'm thrilled to be a part of the 2020 continuity The Fortunes of Texas: Rambling Rose. I not only love this series and the opportunity to meet my favorite recurring characters, but I also enjoy working with some of the most talented Harlequin Special Edition authors. It's fun to plot and brainstorm with the creative women who have become my friends.

In this series, I wrote book three, *The Mayor's Secret Fortune*. If you like reading about tropes such as opposites attract, different worlds, secret pregnancies and marriages of convenience, you're going to enjoy Steven and Ellie's story. Contractor Steven Fortune was born and raised in Florida, but he's looking more like a Texas cowboy each day. He and Mayor Ellie Hernandez have different ideas when it comes to what's best for the town of Rambling Rose, so they constantly bump heads. The only things they agree on are the surprising friendship they form and the growing attraction between them. Ellie is her parents' pride and joy, and her constituents have the utmost respect for their new young mayor. But Ellie's afraid that if—and when—her secret gets out, she's going to disappoint everyone. That is, until Steven offers her a way out.

So fix a cup of coffee or a cold sarsaparilla, then saddle up for a ride into Ellie and Steven's world as you turn the pages of *The Mayor's Secret Fortune*.

Happy reading!

Judy

PS: I love hearing from my readers. You can contact me through my website at judyduarte.com or on Facebook at Facebook.com/JudyDuarteNovelist.

The Mayor's Secret Fortune

Judy Duarte

HARLEQUIN
SPECIAL
EDITION

Special thanks and acknowlegment are given
to Judy Duarte for her contribution to
The Fortunes of Texas: Rambling Rose continuity.

Recycling programs
for this product may
not exist in your area.

ISBN-13: 978-1-335-89441-0

The Mayor's Secret Fortune

Copyright © 2020 by Harlequin Books S.A.

This edition published by arrangement with Harlequin Books S.A.

For questions and comments about the quality of this book,
please contact us at CustomerService@Harlequin.com.

Harlequin Enterprises ULC
22 Adelaide St. West, 40th Floor
Toronto, Ontario M5H 4E3, Canada
www.Harlequin.com

Printed in U.S.A.

Since 2002, *USA TODAY* bestselling author **Judy Duarte** has written over forty books for Harlequin Special Edition, earned two RITA® Award nominations, won two Maggie Awards and received a National Readers' Choice Award. When she's not cooped up in her writing cave, she enjoys traveling with her husband and spending quality time with her grandchildren. You can learn more about Judy and her books on her website, judyduarte.com, or at Facebook.com/judyduartenovelist.

Books by Judy Duarte

Harlequin Special Edition

Rocking Chair Rodeo

Roping in the Cowgirl
The Bronc Rider's Baby
A Cowboy Family Christmas
The Soldier's Twin Surprise
The Lawman's Convenient Family

The Fortunes of Texas: The Secret Fortunes

From Fortune to Family Man

The Fortunes of Texas: The Rulebreakers

No Ordinary Fortune

Return to Brighton Valley

The Daddy Secret
The Bachelor's Brighton Valley Bride
The Soldier's Holiday Homecoming

Visit the Author Profile page
at Harlequin.com for more titles.

To the amazing authors who took part
in The Fortunes of Texas: Rambling Rose—
Michelle Major, Stella Bagwell, Marie Ferrarella,
Nancy Robards Thompson and Allison Leigh.

You ladies rock!
Thank you for making my book a joy to write.

Chapter One

Rain splattered the windshield as Ellie Hernandez maneuvered her recently detailed red Honda through the wet city streets, trying to get to the ribbon-cutting ceremony on time. She was the mayor of Rambling Rose, for goodness' sake. And she always made it a point to arrive at a meeting or an event early. Hopefully, today wasn't the exception.

She glanced at the clock on the dash and rolled her eyes. In fifteen minutes she was supposed to be on hand for the grand opening of the Shoppes, a collection of high-end stores that would cater to the wealthy, a swarm of which had been moving to Rambling Rose in recent months. They'd begun to infiltrate the small town she loved, threatening to make the community in which she'd been raised unrecognizable. And she found the whole thing unsettling.

Not that she didn't want the community to grow and prosper. She believed that growth should be organic, the result of Rambling Rose's quaint, small-town appeal, and not fabricated commercialism.

As the wipers swished and swooshed across the windshield, a big black Dodge Ram passed her on the left, its right rear tire hitting a puddle and splashing a wave of muddy water at the side of her car so high that it struck the windshield with a vengeance.

"Hey, jerk! Watch where you're going." She didn't recognize the fancy, late-model vehicle, so she assumed it was one of the rich newcomers, no doubt in a hurry to join in the excitement of yet another one of Fortune Brothers Construction's grand openings.

Callum, Steven and Dillon Fortune had come to Texas eager to make their mark in real estate renovation. Sure, Ellie could appreciate them renovating the old foundling hospital, which was now the Rambling Rose Pediatric Center. And the new veterinary clinic they'd opened last month would benefit the community, too. But the locals, the people who'd made their homes here long before the big real estate boom, weren't into wearing designer clothing. Nor were the small-town masses interested in dining in a five-star restaurant, another of the Fortune Brothers Construction projects.

The rain had stopped, so she shut off her windshield wipers. Moments later, she pulled into the parking lot, just behind the guy driving the black pickup. After finding a spot and shutting off the ignition, she reached for her purse and grabbed her compact red umbrella. Earlier, on the morning news, the weatherman had said the storm was moving south today, but Ellie wasn't going to take any chances.

She climbed out of the car just as the pickup driver—a corporate cowboy, if that fancy black hat was a clue—got out of his vehicle, too. She paid him little mind. Being on time, to her, meant arriving at least fifteen minutes early, and the clock was ticking relentlessly.

Still, her late arrival couldn't be helped. She'd had a doctor's appointment at ten o'clock, but he was running behind. And now she was, too. Running, that is.

As she hurried toward the entrance, making her way around a couple of puddles, she wished she'd worn something more sensible than heels, like the pair of sneakers packed in the gym bag she always kept in her trunk. But she favored business attire while working on behalf of city hall, and even when she'd had to squeeze in a visit to the doctor, she hadn't wanted to take the extra time to change shoes.

In her peripheral vision, she spotted the approaching cowboy, all tall and lean and...

Fortune.

Steven, to be exact.

She'd known that he and his brothers, Callum and Dillon, would be here today. The Florida developers had moved to Rambling Rose last fall with visions of grandeur that had already begun to change the once blue-collar town for good. And the Shoppes was another one of their fixer-upper projects.

She couldn't help but glance to her right, and when she did, Steven tipped the brim of his black Stetson and tossed a dazzling smile her way.

She offered him a polite but forced smile of her own and picked up her pace, her heels clicking on the newly paved blacktop in a don't-be-late cadence. But she couldn't seem to shake him.

"Good afternoon, Mayor," he said, his voice deep and almost booming. "What's your hurry? We're nearly ten minutes early."

"I know, but that feels late to me." She tried to ignore his tall, dark and handsome presence, but that was nearly impossible to do, especially when it seemed that those big blue eyes of his had a permanent spark in them.

In the five or six months since Steven had moved to town, he seemed to always stand out in the crowd. He'd also acquired a sexy cowboy swagger. If she didn't know better, she'd think he'd been born and bred in Texas rather than in Florida.

Now, as he moved beside her, close enough for her to catch a whiff of his musky aftershave, one of his long strides matching two of hers, people were going to think they'd arrived together. Maybe even in the same vehicle.

Great. Just great. Not that any of the Fortune brothers was her nemesis. It's just that they didn't see eye to eye with her on much of anything, and she had a responsibility to the people who'd voted her into office—the hardworking citizens who'd lived here for years and weren't comfortable with the influx of wealthy newcomers. So, needless to say, arriving with Steven at her side made it look as if she and Fortune Brothers Construction were in cahoots. And that wasn't the case.

Still as much as she hated to admit it, rich or poor, Steven was far more attractive than a man had a right to be. And a misplaced attraction like that was the last thing she needed today.

No, there were more important things to think about than the sexy man sauntering next to her— like the short speech she had to make in a few minutes. On top of that, she had a lot to ponder after today's exam at the doctor's office. As a result, she wasn't paying attention to the rain-slicked ground, and her foot slipped on something wet and hard—a small rock or stone? She let out a little shriek as she lost her balance.

Steven reached out to catch her. Before the wannabe hero could save the day—or prevent her from making a clumsy fool of herself—she landed on her backside with a wet, muddy thud that sent her hair clip flying across the ground as cold, dirty water soaked through her slacks to her panties.

"Are you okay?" Steven asked.

"I'm fine." She brushed a loose strand of hair from her face and tucked it behind her ear. For a moment, her tummy flip-flopped, and she feared she'd be sick. But she sucked in a breath of fresh air, and the feeling soon passed.

Steven reached down to take her hand, his brow furrowed, his eyes…

Dammit. The sympathetic gaze and the sky-blue color were almost enough to chase the clouds away. Almost.

In spite of her reluctance to accept his help, she took his hand, feeling the warmth as it embraced hers. Work roughened, yet soft and gentle at the same time.

From her position on the ground, he appeared much taller than six foot something. The moment he pulled her to a stand, her legs wobbled, and her heart rate, already escalated, skipped to a zippity-do-dah beat.

"There you go," he said, his smile as nice as it could be—yet, under the circumstances, annoying all the same.

She drew her hand from his and cleared her throat. "Thank you."

"Are you sure you're okay?" he asked.

Ellie blew out a sigh. "I'm actually more humiliated than hurt."

Could anything else go wrong today? It didn't seem likely.

She brushed her wet derriere and realized she couldn't get on a stage looking like a drowned rat—and no doubt, one of the last to leave a sinking ship. Her town was a-changin', and there wasn't one darn thing she could do about it.

As she turned to head back to her car, where she kept her handy-dandy Ellie Hernandez Emergency Preparedness Kit, a sharp twinge shot through her ankle. Her steps faltered, and she swore under her breath.

"Let me help." Steven took her by the arm, his grip strong and steady, yet tender.

Another woman might appreciate the gallant gesture—or be flattered by it—but Ellie pulled away and waved him off. "Thanks, but I've got this."

All she had to do was figure out where the nearest bathroom was so she could change into one of the two spare outfits she always had with her. As she limped back toward her car, past the vehicles that had arrived earlier, she reached into her purse, pulled out her key fob and, using the remote, popped open her trunk.

"What are you doing?" he asked.

"Getting something to change into." She removed a neatly folded pair of slacks and a matching blouse she kept in the car for spur-of-the-moment business meetings or unscheduled events, then grabbed her gym bag.

Steven let out a slow whistle. "Would you look at that? You keep a traveling wardrobe on hand. I'm impressed."

"I like being prepared." The irony, though, struck her with a low blow. She could count a handful of times in recent months that she hadn't been the least bit prepared for the unexpected.

"Where do you plan to change clothes?" he asked.

She shot him an incredulous look. "In a bathroom. Why?"

"I have a much better idea—and one that's quicker. Our construction trailer is about fifty yards from here. Think you can make it?"

She paused only a moment before nodding and falling into step beside him.

As much as she hated to accept any help from one of the Fortune brothers, she'd much rather change in a trailer than one of the nearby porta-potties, which would be her only alternative if she didn't want to do so in her car or, God forbid, trek through the gathering crowd with wet pants and dirty hands to search for a restroom inside the Shoppes.

She glanced at her bangle wristwatch. "I can't believe this is happening. I'm never late."

"Relax," he said. "They're not going to start the grand opening without either one of us."

He was right, of course. But all Ellie needed was for someone to see them enter that blasted trailer together and think the worst. Talk about sleeping with the enemy. How was she going to spin her way out of this?

After Steven unlocked the door to the trailer to let Ellie inside, she turned to him and scrunched her pretty face.

"You're going to wait out here, right?"

"Of course. If you feel more comfortable, use the lock."

She stepped inside, and the door snapped shut. The sound of the dead bolt followed.

"Seriously?" Steven muttered.

"I heard that!"

Steven slowly shook his head as he stood on the wooden porch steps, holding the company keys and waiting for the pretty but disheveled mayor to change. He sucked in a deep breath of the rain-scented air and scanned the sky. Storm clouds, once dark and threatening, had lightened and begun to move on, giving way to small patches of blue. Thank goodness the people who'd shown up for today's ceremony wouldn't get drenched.

He'd been looking forward to the ribbon-cutting ceremony at the Shoppes at Rambling Rose for months. It was the third grand opening Fortune Brothers Construction had held this year. And with each one, their reputation back in Florida, as well as in Texas, grew stronger and more impressive.

Too bad that wasn't the case here, in Rambling Rose. You'd think the town council and Mayor Ellie Hernandez would be happy that Steven and his brothers had remodeled the old five-and-dime. Once an eyesore that had been abandoned and neglected for more than twenty years, it was now an elegant two-story building that housed a variety of upscale boutiques. But for some damned reason, she didn't consider their contribution to the community.

Last month, at the fund-raiser for the new Paws and Claws Animal Clinic, Ellie had made it clear that she wasn't impressed with the progressive changes he and his brothers had made, or were making, to the town.

Steven lifted his left wrist and glanced at his Rolex, a birthday gift from his father. It was nearly time to get the show on the road, although he'd meant what he'd told Ellie when they arrived—the ribbon cutting wouldn't take place without them. Still, her little misstep was bound to be a setback.

She might keep spare clothing packed neatly in her trunk, but that didn't mean she'd change faster than any other woman who made it a point to have every hair in place. And as far as Steven was concerned, the tall, willowy brunette looked damn near perfect each time he saw her.

A slow grin stretched across his face. Seeing Ms. Perfection seated in a mud puddle, her hair hanging wild and loose instead of contained in a neat twist, her sable eyes wide and lips parted in disbelief, was a pretty sight to behold. And a far cry from the image the good folks of Rambling Rose had come to know and love.

From what he'd gathered, Ellie had been an only child, her mama and daddy's pride and joy. She'd sold more cookies than any of the others in her Girl Scout troop, sung solos in the church choir and helped the women's club serve meals at the home-less shelter. She'd gone on to become the valedic-

torian of her senior class before earning a master's
in public policy. So it wasn't just her pretty face
that was impressive.

Still, she seemed a little too good to be true, too
damn perfect. He wondered what flaws might be
lurking beneath the surface. There had to be something, if only he could find it. He also needed to
get on her good side, but so far, he hadn't had any
luck with either of those tasks.

Steven leaned against the wooden porch railing,
prepared to wait it out. When the door squeaked
open, taking him a bit by surprise, Ellie breezed
out of the trailer, smiling as if she'd never suf-
fered a setback. The only sign of being flustered
was her flushed cheeks, which merely added a
rosy tint to her olive complexion and made her
brown eyes pop.

"Thank you," she said. "Changing in the Fortune Brothers Construction man cave was a lot
nicer than using one of the porta-potties."

"You're welcome." He tossed her a disarming
smile, which seemed to escape her notice. On the
other hand, her appearance didn't escape his.

She'd come outside different—not just from
when she went in, but from when she'd arrived.
She'd combed her hair, leaving it down instead of
in her customary updo, and she'd changed out of
the dressy black pants she'd had on, trading them

for khaki slacks. She'd shed her tailored jacket and the crisply pressed white blouse, too. Instead she wore a cream-colored sweater accessorized with a red plaid scarf.

"Just look at you," he said. "A little more casual and down-to-earth than when you arrived, but as professionally dressed as ever."

He'd meant it as a compliment, but she never seemed to be sure about him or his true intentions, so it didn't surprise him when she rolled her eyes and clicked her tongue. "Under the circumstances, it's the best I could do."

"Nicely done, then."

"Thank you," she said, "but let's *go*."

At that, she took off, walking past him while he locked up and leaving him to catch an intriguing hint of her citrus-blossom scent.

After slipping the keys into his jeans pocket, he followed her, enjoying the sway of her hips and the way her long, dark hair swished across her back—a very nice change. She really ought to wear it down more often.

He shook off his thoughts and caught up with her.

In spite of a slight limp the pair of gym shoes couldn't mask, she never broke stride.

"What time is it?" she asked.

"Like I said, they'll wait."

She let out a huff. "That's *not* the point."

They stopped by her car long enough for her to toss her gym bag into the back seat, the hasty effort a sign of her inner frustration.

"Why do I get the distinct feeling you don't like me?" he asked.

At that, her movements finally stilled. "I don't have any reason to dislike *you*. It's just that the changes you and your brothers have been making in Rambling Rose aren't helping the community at large. And it's clear that you don't know the townspeople well enough to give a damn what they want."

"You're wrong. My brothers and I care about the residents of Rambling Rose."

Ellie chuffed. "You only care about the newcomers. Now that the homes in Rambling Rose Estates have gone on the market, we've had an influx of millionaires move in. And the longtime residents feel pushed out. Unappreciated."

"The locals might not like the idea of new residents moving in—wealthy or not. But you can't blame Fortune Brothers Construction for the hard feelings."

She didn't respond in words, but her arched brow clearly said, *Oh no? Who else is to blame?*

"When Bradley Industries came in with big dreams and then went belly-up, my brother and I picked up the pieces and finished projects in record time. I'd think you'd be happy that someone was able to complete them."

She didn't comment. But what could she say?

The way Steven saw it, Fortune Brothers Construction had stepped in and made the community a better place. "You have to admit that our recent renovations of the pediatric center and the animal clinic will benefit everyone in Rambling Rose."

"Maybe so." She nodded toward the elegant, two-story glass-front entrance to the Shoppes. "But what about this? Just look at this place."

"What's wrong with it? It looks great." And hell, why wouldn't he think that? He'd helped design it.

She slapped her hands on her hips. "The people who live in Rambling Rose, the ones who were born and raised here, aren't that fancy. They don't shop in stores like this. Nor do they appreciate the fact that, thanks to all the wealthy newcomers, the owners stand to turn a big enough profit to allow them to afford the rent in a luxurious setting. And that will create larger social and economic divisions in our communities, something we've never had before, which is my point."

"I appreciate your loyalty to your constituents and your desire to keep things the way they've always been, but the world is changing, Ellie. The technology-savvy millennials prefer specialty shops over department stores—or else they're shopping online."

The attractive mayor, Ms. Perfection, practically snorted. "I'm a millennial, Steven. And I'm not impressed by fancy buildings and expensive specialty shops."

He merely studied her. He admired her passion for the town as it used to be. And he found her more than a little intriguing. He wasn't exactly sure how old she was—late twenties, he assumed. Either way, she seemed too young to be a mayor, even of a small town like Rambling Rose.

When he didn't respond right away, she took a deep breath and slowly let it out. "I'm sorry. I didn't mean to put us at odds before the ceremony."

"No worries. I'm not the least bit offended." In spite of their difference of opinion, he actually enjoyed their banter.

He'd grown up as the oldest son of a very wealthy man, and while he and his siblings were all accomplished, the brothers had built the construction company to the point that they'd each become financially successful in their own rights. So Steven was used to being catered to, flirted with and pursued by attractive women.

But that wasn't the case with Ellie, and he found that refreshing. She intrigued him. Yet it was more than her spunky attitude he found appealing. He'd always been attracted to brunettes, and this one had caught his interest the very first time he'd laid eyes her.

"We can talk later," she said. "We need to climb up on that stage and get this event over with." And with that, she was off once again.

A car door slammed shut, and Steven glanced across the parking lot, where several men and women had gathered around a white SUV, its rear door lifted high. There didn't seem to be anything unusual about the vehicle, but there was something out of sync about the people.

When one guy reached into the back and began to hand out signs, Steven realized why.

Protesters. That's all they needed.

Had Ellie spotted them? Apparently not, since she continued toward the makeshift dais, where a red ribbon stretched across the front of the glass doors.

Then again, maybe she had inside information and had known they'd be here. If she didn't have to attend the grand opening in an official capacity, she might have held one of the protest signs herself. She clearly shared their sentiments. But if there was one thing Steven had come to know about Ellie Hernandez, it was that she took her job as mayor seriously.

That being the case, would she go so far as to shut down the protesters or call in law enforcement?

Another car door slammed, and three more people joined the first group. He suspected all hell
was about to break loose. Steven and his brothers
could handle anything they might throw their way.
But how was the pretty young mayor of Rambling
Rose going to respond, especially if things were
to blow sky-high and a fight broke out?

Steven hated to admit it, but he couldn't wait
to find out.

Chapter Two

Ellie had been tempted to suggest that Steven wait in the parking lot for a minute or two so they could stagger their arrival, but since he seemed determined to stick by her side, she figured he'd refuse. So she gave up her efforts to shake the sexy man who looked more like a fancy cowboy than a slick businessman.

As they neared the front of the Shoppes, her steps slowed to a casual pace, and she tucked a loose strand of hair behind her ear. Up ahead, a crowd had gathered around the portable dais, where a well-dressed Callum Fortune stood off to the side, near a small table, checking his watch.

Two women in their mid- to late fifties turned when they heard approaching footsteps and eyed Ellie and Steven carefully, as if connecting imaginary dots and jumping to the wrong conclusion.

"Great," Ellie uttered softly. "I knew they'd think we'd arrived together."

"So what?" he asked. "Who cares?"

"I do. It's bad enough that I have to stand next to you and your brother on that dais as if we were all in agreement."

"Sleeping with the enemy, huh?"

That thought had crossed her mind more than once, and while the thought of sleeping with a man like Steven Fortune knocked her a little off stride, she stopped to set him straight.

"I'm a city official," she said, "and my loyalty lies with my constituents."

He flashed a dazzling, heart-strumming grin. "I moved to Rambling Rose back in October, so that makes me one of your constituents."

"Point taken, but for now, we have a grand opening to officiate." She offered the two women gawking at them a polite smile, then hurried toward the portable dais, with Steven matching her strides.

The moment Callum noticed them, he motioned for them to join him and Dillon on stage. Ellie blew out a sigh. Did they have to make a big Broadway production out of everything? Not that there hadn't been other grand openings in town, but the folks in Rambling Rose kept things simple, and they served punch and cookies at the end.

As she and Steven climbed the side steps to the dais, her stomach pitched. She sucked in another comforting breath, which served to settle her nerves, as well as her tummy.

Callum removed a handheld microphone from a small table and addressed the crowd. "On behalf of Fortune Brothers Construction and all the store owners, I'd like to welcome you to the grand opening of the Shoppes at Rambling Rose."

Several people clapped heartily, most of them newcomers. But the ones Ellie recognized in the small crowd had a more reserved response.

"My brothers and I are happy to be a part of Rambling Rose's renaissance," Callum said as he handed the mic to Steven. Ellie, who'd taken her place to the left of the men, slapped on another polite smile and stood with her hands clasped behind her back.

"I've only been in town for the past four or five months," Steven said, "but in that short period of time, I feel as though I've become part of the community." He glanced at Ellie as if hoping she'd back him up, but she'd already gone above and beyond to do her job today—and to keep her thoughts and opinions to herself.

Most of them, anyway. She hadn't wanted to

put a damper on the festivities, especially since the rain had stopped.

Callum handed Steven a stack of gold-trimmed envelopes, then picked up the scissors Ellie would use to cut the red ribbon that stretched across the doorway leading to the stores.

"As a gift from Fortune Brothers Construction," Steven said, "as well as the store owners and eateries, each of you will be given coupons for discounts on today's purchases and a chance to win prizes."

At that, the crowd cheered and clapped.

"So without further ado," Steven said, "we'll ask Mayor Hernandez to cut the ribbon so you can go inside and meet the newest members of the Rambling Rose Chamber of Commerce."

Steven gave Callum the mic, exchanging it for the scissors, but before he could pass them to Ellie, a male voice shouted, "Fortunes, go home!"

She didn't have to see the man who'd interrupted the grand opening. She recognized Mel Sullivan's graveled voice. The woolly, white-haired man was one of the older townspeople and a regular at the Roadside Diner, as well as at Mariana's Market. Mel had been voicing his opinions loud and clear for months, and since he stood front and center of the group of protesters, he appeared to be the ringleader. She also recognized the others with him, six to the right and four to the left, all

carrying hand-painted signs as they moved forward and approached the dais.

"Rambling Rose doesn't need any more of those
highfalutin rich people parading around town and
showing off their wealth," Carl Wagner shouted.
"Send 'em packing, and tell them to take their
money with 'em."

Ruthanne Garrison cried out, "Save our town,
Mayor!"

That's it. Enough was enough. Ellie snatched
the microphone from Steven and took center stage.
"Friends, neighbors, I understand your concern,
and I support your First Amendment rights, but
the people gathered here today have every right
to go shopping without any trouble or turmoil."

Ellie handed the mic to Steven. "You cut the
ribbon. I'm going to talk to them."

"Want me to go with you?" he asked.

She slowly shook her head. "That would only
make things worse." Then she turned and made
her way down the steps to speak to the people she
considered her friends and, hopefully, convince
them to get into their cars and go home.

Mel, Carl, Ruthanne and the others were all
good people—and well-intentioned. She'd known
them all her life, and they'd watched her grow up.
They trusted her to send the Fortunes packing and
to save their quaint town from further ruin.

Hopefully, she wouldn't let them down. At least,

not with respect to the Fortunes. But the time was coming when she'd have to humbly face the community at large and reveal her secret.

She cringed at the thought of letting them down, of admitting that she'd failed to live up to everyone's expectations. Ever since childhood, she'd tried to be perfect and had worked hard to develop a respectable reputation. And up until now, she'd succeeded. But she'd recently made a big mistake, and she would soon have to deal with the repercussions.

A few of the townspeople might not give it another thought. Yet some would be shocked and others disappointed to learn that in five short months, Ellie Hernandez, hometown superstar, would become an unwed mother with no husband in sight.

The glass-enclosed lobby of the Shoppes wasn't especially large, but it was certainly fancy, boasting a colorful Spanish-tile waterfall in the center of the room that had been created by a Texas artisan. Even the floor tile provided a rich look that would appeal to the wealthy newcomers.

The Fortunes had gone to great lengths to lay out a remarkable welcome to the potential shoppers. They'd set a variety of refreshments on several linen-draped tables, each adorned with orchids and other exotic floral arrangements that had been provided by Tropical Paradise, the new flower shop located on the lower level.

Servers dressed in black slacks and crisply-pressed, tailored white shirts carried silver trays, some of which held flutes filled with champagne or sparkling apple cider, while others displayed a variety of fancy hors d'oeuvres. Ellie chose to pass on everything, especially since she hadn't quite kicked the morning sickness that had plagued her early in her pregnancy.

A woman in her thirties, who stood with a group of friends, opened her gold-lined envelope and let out a happy shriek. "Oh my gosh! I won a pair of jade earrings from Sebastian's Fine Jewelry."

The server carrying the goose-liver pâté walked by, close enough for Ellie to get a tummy-swirling whiff. She quickly took a step back and turned toward the fountain, hoping she wouldn't have to run to the restroom. She swallowed hard, took a deep breath of fresh air, cooled and cleansed by gurgling water, then stepped to the side and turned her back to the server.

"There you are."

Ellie looked up and spotted Steven sauntering toward her, carrying two flutes of champagne. He handed one to her, but she slowly shook her head. "Thank you, but I'll pass."

"Seriously?" he asked.

She actually liked champagne and would have accepted a glass, had she not been pregnant. She also could have held on to it, pretending to take part in the festivities, but she wasn't in the mood to fake it.

"Come on, Ellie. Lighten up. Can't you think of anything to celebrate?"

"I'm here, aren't I?" She offered him a smile that was more sincere than any of the others she'd managed on prior occasions when their paths had crossed.

Steven's smile faded, as if he might be slightly offended—or bothered. Or…?

Oh, for heaven's sake. Who knew what a rich man like Steven Fortune ever really had on his mind? Even his last name screamed wealth.

"It's not what you think," she said. "It's just that I need to keep a clear head while I'm on the job."

At that, his grin returned, recreating a pair of dimples that threatened to unravel her. And Ellie rarely let things get to her. She glanced at her wristwatch. Had she stayed at the grand opening long enough? Could she find an excuse to cut out now?

As one of the servers walked by with several more flutes, Steven motioned for the man to come over.

"Here," he told the server, as he placed one of the glasses back on the silver tray. "Can I trade you for one of the apple ciders?"

"Absolutely, Mr. Fortune." He reached for a single flute, its contents a bit darker than the rest, and gave it to him. "Here you go, sir."

Steven thanked him, then handed the sparkling juice to Ellie and lifted his glass of champagne in a toast. "To Rambling Rose."

She would have been hard-pressed to join him in celebrating the Fortune brothers' latest venture, but how could she not drink to the town she loved?

She clinked her glass to his, setting off the rich, resonating sound of fine crystal, which only served to remind her of the wealth that threatened to turn her beloved Rambling Rose into a metropolis.

Still, she took a sip of the sweet bubbly.

What would Steven say if she told him the real reason she'd passed on an alcoholic drink? Not that it mattered. He'd find out soon enough. And so would her parents.

Her gut clenched at the thought of the loving couple she'd tried so hard to make proud. It would kill her to see the disappointment in their eyes.

"Hey," Steven said, "what's with the turned-up nose? Did you get a bad pour? Bitter champagne instead of sweet cider?"

Ellie hadn't meant to let her thoughts alter her expression, let alone her demeanor, especially at a public event. So she forced a carefree grin and tried to laugh it off. "No, the drink is fine. *I'm* fine. It's just that I… Well, a weird thought crossed my mind, and I drifted off for a moment. That's all. No big deal."

But it wasn't just a fleeting thought that had stolen her away from the present and set off a flurry of concern. It was cold, hard reality. And once her tummy bulge turned into a full-on baby bump, it was actually going to be a big deal. A *huge* one.

Ellie had never backed down from a challenge, but this one scared her silly. After the truth came out and she experienced her fall from grace, there'd be more than a few awkward or embarrassing moments. Sure, they'd soon fade and life would go on. But there was something else she found troubling, something she'd need to deal with. Because, when push came to shove, she wasn't sure if she could handle the mayorship and motherhood. But that's the last thing in the world she'd ever reveal to Steven.

"I want to show you something," he said.

Huh? Her brow twitched, and her head tilted. As their gazes met and locked, something stirred inside her, drawing her out of her uneasy thoughts and—

"Come with me." He nodded toward the farthest corner of the festive lobby, where three large brass easels held a couple of fancy poster boards displaying several other projects Fortune Brothers Construction had in the works.

She couldn't very well refuse to look at the exhibit of their future renovations, so she followed him to the impressive, professional presentation.

Steven pointed to the first poster. "This is Paz, the wellness spa we'll be opening soon."

Ellie studied the sketch of the exterior of a beautiful building.

"It's going to be finished with reclaimed wood and other natural materials," he added.

"Nice."

"That's it?" He feigned disbelief. "You can't tell me that a busy mayor like you wouldn't need to unwind once in a while at a luxurious spa."

Of course she would. And she'd love it. But she didn't want him to think he'd won her over, so she gave a little shrug. "I'm really not what you'd call the luxurious type."

"I don't believe that. Everyone needs a good massage once in a while." He lifted his hands and moved his fingers in a kneading fashion, as if they were working their magic on an invisible body. "I'm sure you have plenty of stress built up and have a few knots. Or maybe you just need to relax. If not, you should just be pampered."

The thought of his hands on her body sent her senses reeling and her imagination soaring.

Oh, for Pete's sake, Ellie. Cut it out. What's the matter with you?

No way would she let those hands anywhere

near her—no matter how good she imagined they'd feel.

She moved to the middle easel, hoping to dispel any pampering thoughts—his or hers—and studied the next drawing.

"That's the restaurant," Steven said. "Callum found the property in January."

"The old feed store?"

"Yes. Ashley, Megan and Nicole were in town for Callum and Becky's wedding, and when they saw the building and property, they jumped on the idea. We've already started the renovations. They're going to call it Provisions. They have a lot of experience in upscale restaurants, so I know it's going to be popular."

"When will it open?"

"If all goes well, it should open in May, so they're eager to move to Rambling Rose so they can get busy."

Great. More Fortunes would be moving to town. Not that Ellie had anything against the family—especially the sisters she'd never met. It's just that there'd be three more wealthy people moving here.

Unable to help herself, Ellie asked, "How many sisters do you have?"

"Four. Stephanie is already here and working at Paws and Claws. And the triplets make four."

Triplets? Ellie nearly rolled her eyes. Goodness. They came in multiples. Her hand slipped to her tummy. Thank goodness she was only expecting one baby. What would she do with three?

She shook off the overwhelming thought, then took a step to her right and focused on the last easel, which displayed the plans for and a sketch of the Fortune Hotel.

"I'm surprised you and your brothers decided to promote the sketches of this project," she said.

"Why?" Steven crossed his arms, shifted his weight to one hip and tossed her a dazzling grin. "Just because we've met a little resistance from the Rambling Rose planning commission?"

"A *little*?" She returned his smile, although hers was smug.

"Let's just call that a snag," he said. "And a little inconvenience for the time being. We'll break ground soon, and it'll be up and running before you know it. Think of the property taxes that'll be coming in. Believe me, once local business owners begin to see the increased revenue brought in by tourists and visitors, the community will not only accept it, but they'll be proud of it, too."

"Don't be too sure about that," she said.

"Why?"

"Because it's not just about the money. The locals aren't happy about the way you and your family are trying to change our way of life. I told you and your brother as much at the fund-raiser for the new animal clinic, but my words and the point I was trying to make obviously fell on deaf ears."

"Oh, we heard you. Loud and clear. But no one succeeds by thinking small."

She was tempted to call him on the conceit hidden within his statement, but she bit her tongue and addressed the project that wasn't likely to pass the planning commission—*ever*. At least, as long as she was mayor, even if the length of her term was questionable at best.

She turned toward Steven, crossed her arms and strengthened her stance. "You're going to have difficulty getting that project to pass, because it's not going to benefit many of my constituents."

"Change is good."

"That's sometimes true. Just for the record, I'm not opposed to progress, but only if a project maintains Rambling Rose's character. And a sprawling hotel complex fits our town like a pair of Mommy's high heels on a preschooler playing house."

Steven glanced down at her feet, then looked up and grinned. "Or like a pair of sneakers on the mayor?"

"Very funny."

"Like it or not," he said, "the town's character is changing, Ellie. And I think you'd better try to grow with the times. Your constituents will appreciate it in the long run."

She blew out a sigh that released only a bit of

her frustration. "What do you know about the people who voted me into office? I doubt that you've met any of them while living in that big fancy mansion of yours."

"That's probably true."

Instead of a response, she continued to stare at him, although the longer she gazed into those big blue eyes, the less she felt like arguing her point.

Damn him. Steven Fortune might be one gorgeous hunk, but he had a way of blowing the wind out of her sails. In fact, he'd become a real pain in her backside. And the fact that he seemed to enjoy their banter didn't help.

Footsteps sounded, and she glanced over her shoulder to see Steven's brother Callum approach. Other than their six feet or more height and close-cropped dark hair, the two men didn't really resemble each other. They were, however, business partners and shared the same vision.

"Am I interrupting something?" Callum asked, his brown eyes glimmering with mirth.

"Only a stalemate, it seems." Steven winked at Ellie, the playful gesture tempting her to punch him in the arm.

"Why don't you take the mayor on a private tour?" Callum suggested.

Steven gave his brother a cursory glance before locking his gaze on Ellie. "I don't think she wants one. She's not happy about the new stores opening up."

At that, Ellie bristled and felt the need to defend her stance. "I have nothing against the businesses or their owners. It's just that the locals, the ones who were born and raised here, aren't into designer handbags, five-hundred-dollar outfits, French pastries or artisanal cheeses."

"That's yet to be seen," Steven said. "I'll bet some of those folks will end up surprising you."

The man just wasn't getting it. She turned to appeal to his brother instead. "I'll admit that Fortune Brothers Construction has made some improvements to the town, like renovating the old foundling hospital and turning it into a pediatric clinic." In fact, Ellie would be taking her baby boy for checkups with one of the doctors there before she knew it.

"Don't forget about Paws and Claws," Steven said.

"We do have a lot of animal owners," Ellie said. "In fact, last month, at the Valentine's Day fundraiser, my best friend and roommate spent most of the evening checking out the pets available for adoption that night and felt sorry for a scraggly dog with feet that were too big for its little body. So she brought him home right then and there. She named him Tank because of his big paws, but he's practically doubled in size already and has been chewing up everything in the house, including my new sunglasses."

Steven laughed, a mesmerizing sound that lightened Ellie's mood considerably.

"Your friend didn't know she'd adopted a puppy? I'd think someone from Paws and Claws would have made it clear that Tank wouldn't stay small before letting her take him home."

"I'm sure Daria was told—or had figured it out herself. But knowing her, she just didn't care."

"I'd like to meet Tank. And Daria."

Yeah. Right. As if Ellie would invite the irritating but sexy hunk to her home.

"Why would you want to meet that sweet, goofy pup?" she asked. "Is it because he's been creating havoc in my peaceful house?"

"Yep. That's exactly why. It sounds like Tank and I have something in common. We both annoy you, but if you give us a chance, you'll probably find us likable."

Callum laughed and gave his brother a pat on the back. "I don't know about that. Puppies can be trained. And I'm not so sure about you."

"I'd tend to agree with you about that," Ellie said, unable to stifle a smile.

"Becky just arrived." Callum nodded toward the lobby entrance. "Our sitter was running late, so we had to drive over here separately. I'll leave you two to fight it out on your own."

Ellie watched Callum's new wife, a pediatric nurse, step through the glass doorway. Becky had been a single mom—to one-year-old twins. Surely if she'd been able to handle two babies at once, Ellie could handle one. Right?

A little niggle that felt a lot like panic began to stir inside her. Babies were small and vulnerable. And as an only child, she'd never been around them.

She'd only held one once, a long time ago, but the mother had hovered around her as if she was going to drop it or do something wrong. What if she…?

No, Ellie. Chill. You've got this.

As Callum sauntered toward his wife, Steven seemed intent upon returning to the conversation they'd been having.

"You've already admitted that some of our projects have benefited the community," he said.

"Yes, but you and your brother bought up every piece of property you could, and from all outward appearances, you're only focused on what the newest residents want."

"I beg to differ."

Of course he did. She wouldn't expect anything less.

"I'm afraid we'll have to agree to disagree," Ellie said.

"Good idea." His grin morphed into a dimpled

smile. "But if you could do anything—pie in the sky—what changes would you like to see in Rambling Rose?"

She paused for a moment, but not because she didn't have a response, but because the question came from him, and he seemed to be interested in what she had to say.

"I'd start by building a community center that would cover a lot of needs for those who are on a limited income, like senior citizens and single parents. I'd love to see us offer after-school care for latchkey kids, as well as tutoring. And it would be awesome if we could provide classes that would appeal to adults, too, like computer basics, flower arranging, cake decorating, financial planning, yoga, line dancing, pickle ball, which I hear is all the rage. Anyway, you get the idea."

"I do. And I can't make promises without talking to my brothers, but I think we'd all be better off—Rambling Rose, Fortune Brothers Construction—if we could find a way to meet in the middle."

Ellie knew he might be blowing smoke as a way to appease her, so she studied the man, his expression sincere, hopeful. His face so blasted handsome. And she couldn't help but wish that they could find some common ground, but so far, it hadn't seemed possible.

"Would you be willing to meet a few of the

locals and get to know them on their own turf?" she asked. "If so, that would be meeting me in the middle."

"You bet I will. Maybe you can set up a committee—"

She held up the palm of her hand like a traffic cop, stopping him in midthought, and shook her head. "No way. I'm not talking about a meeting down at city hall. I didn't get to be the mayor by forming committees. If you really want to know what makes Rambling Rose tick, you'll need to go where the locals go."

Steven cocked his head slightly. "All right. I'm game. Where do you suggest I meet them? The Grange Hall? The local church?"

"If you really want to get to know the folks who live here, you'll need to go to Mariana's Market on a Saturday morning."

"I've heard about it. Vaguely. But I don't know where that is. Or what it is. Help me out, okay?"

Darn him. He couldn't pull off a meet-and-greet like that without her, and the fact that he was willing to take a field trip away from his fancy home and busy office actually made her eager to facilitate the little excursion.

"You won't find Mariana's Market on your GPS," she said. "Just meet me at my office on Saturday and I'll take you there. Bring your brothers, too."

"All right. You've got a deal." He reached out to shake her hand, and as his long fingers slipped around hers in a warm, firm grip, her senses reeled as if…

As if *nothing*, she admonished herself.

Ellie glanced at her wristwatch while trying to come up with a plausible reason to cut out and go home.

"As much as I'm enjoying our chat," she said, "I really need to go. I promised my roommate that I'd puppy-sit."

"And I really should greet my sister-in-law, as well as the other guests and shopkeepers. But I'll see you on Saturday." He tossed her another dazzling smile that darn near melted her in place. Then he turned and sauntered away.

Ellie watched him go, torn between admiration for the guy and frustration with his plans to ruin her town.

Too bad the Fortunes hadn't remained in Fort Lauderdale, doing whatever the rich and famous did there. Yacht races, maybe. Sunning themselves on the white sands of the Atlantic. And what a sight that would be for tourists and Floridians alike.

Unable to stop herself, she sought Steven in the crowd once again.

Unlike Callum, Steven had quickly shed his no-worries, Tommy Bahama style. And with each week he remained in Texas, the more he seemed to have acquired a cowboy persona—albeit a cowboy with more money than he knew what to do with.

And now it seemed she'd have to come face-to-face with him on a regular basis, especially if the construction company continued to have ribbon-cutting ceremonies every time she turned around. She'd take Steven and his brothers to Mariana's, although she wasn't sure that would have the desired effect on any of the Fortunes.

But try as she might, she couldn't quite shake the desire or the effect Steven Fortune threatened to have on her.

Chapter Three

On Saturday morning, Steven rode shotgun in Ellie's Honda while his brother Dillon sat in the back, a rather nondescript expression on his face. At twenty-nine, the fair-haired, blue-eyed Fortune brother was the kind of man most women would find attractive. At least, when he smiled. But he hadn't been doing too much of that lately.

Steven had invited Callum to join them on the expedition to Mariana's Market, but Callum had passed. He and Becky had taken the twins to the Austin Zoo today. Steven thought the toddlers were a little too young for a trip like that, but both

Callum and Becky had seemed excited about the family outing.

Of course, that just went to show you how little Steven knew about babies—or modern parenting. Their father, David Fortune, might have been a good dad and a great financial provider, but he'd left the daily child-rearing tasks to their mom. And when their mother's health issues struck with a vengeance, the boys had had to look after their younger sisters. Callum had made it clear that he'd grown tired of the responsibility. That fact coupled with a rocky first marriage that ended in divorce, he'd been reluctant to have a family of his own and had been hesitant to get involved with a single mother.

Before meeting Becky, Callum had put the construction company and business first. But he fell in love with the pretty, kindhearted nurse, and she'd left her mark on him, making him a new man. Not that the change wasn't a good one. It's just that Steven was still getting used to seeing his brother carrying toddlers, wiping noses and changing diapers. The guy even seemed to enjoy it.

Steven wasn't going to swear off having kids or a family, but if and when the day came, he wasn't going to take such a hands-on approach to fatherhood.

He glanced over his shoulder at Dillon, who looked a bit cramped sitting in back. Dillon hadn't complained, but then again, he hadn't said much of anything this morning.

"You doing okay back there?" Steven asked.

"Yeah. Why?"

"You're pretty quiet."

Dillon shrugged a single shoulder. "I don't have anything to say."

Steven shouldn't find that unusual. His brother had been pretty tight-lipped since moving to Rambling Rose. Probably because he'd loved living in Florida and seemed to be having a hard time adjusting to life in Texas.

He occasionally seemed to retreat into himself about something, but on the whole he was a pretty quiet guy, and his brothers hadn't wanted to poke too much.

"You want me to move my seat forward to give you more room?" Steven asked.

"No need. I'm doing all right."

Maybe so. But as Steven turned around and faced the front, he wished he'd insisted that they take his Cadillac Escalade instead of Ellie's sedan. At least the SUV would have provided his brother with more leg room. But Ellie had made it clear that she was running the show today, so he'd let her take the lead.

As they drove down a long rural road, he spotted an abandoned factory up ahead, where a wide variety of trucks and cars parked in an adjacent graveled lot.

Ellie turned on her blinker, indicating a turn into the place, and Steven's brow furrowed. *Seriously?* This was the place where all the locals hung out?

He wasn't sure what he'd expected Mariana's to be—a coffee shop, maybe—but it looked as if Ellie was taking them to a flea market. He scanned the periphery, the shaded tables, the trucks parked with open tailgates that displayed their wares. If these were the locals Ellie had wanted him to meet, he'd have to agree—her constituents weren't likely to shop at high-end stores.

As they got out of the car, Steven turned to his lovely tour director for the day, who'd dressed casually in a pink T-shirt, black jeans and a pair of sneakers. "So this is Mariana's?"

She nodded, a bit smugly.

"I never would have guessed."

At that, she smiled, a bit of pride glimmering in her eyes. "Mariana's Market has been around for as long as the town has. And this is the real deal. Rambling Rose at its best. I wanted you to meet some of the people who've lived here for years, the folks who keep everything running smoothly—mechanics, handymen, waitresses, farmers. You'll even see some of the ranchers who live nearby."

"I live on a ranch," Steven reminded her.

Ellie laughed. "Is *that* what you call it?"

"Okay, so the Fame and Fortune isn't actually a working ranch, if that's what you mean. But we have a stable and horses."

Ellie clicked her tongue. "Oh, come on, Steven. That isn't a house you live in. It's a sprawling mansion with enough space for your entire family to live on the property and still maintain their privacy."

All right. He had to give her that.

As they neared the open-air marketplace, Steven spotted a couple of vendors along the edge, their tables shaded by colorful canopies, as well as a variety of shoppers, all of whom seemed to know each other.

"Mariana's has sure drawn a crowd," Steven said. "What do they sell here?"

"All kinds of things. Vintage clothing, discount perfumes and even some homemade goop that's guaranteed to clean oil leaks off the driveway. You can also buy used furniture and handmade crafts and baked goods. Frances Elliot makes these great hand-knit scarves and sweaters. And Alice McKinley's quilts are amazing. In fact, she's making one to order for me, a shabby-chic style for my bed." Ellie tossed him an enthusiastic smile that put a spark in her pretty brown eyes.

Damn, he could get lost in that sparkly expression.

Were they somehow becoming friends? He hoped so. And not just for business or political reasons.

"Looks like the high school cheerleaders turned out." Dillon pointed to a table where a couple of teenage girls were selling tickets of some kind.

"Rambling Rose High School is having a talent show next week," Ellie said. "It would be a good idea if you and your brothers bought a few tickets in support of the kids."

Steven wasn't so sure he wanted to attend an event like that, but she was right. It would probably help if people saw him and his brothers getting involved in the community, and especially with the youth. So what the hell. "Sure, I'll buy some tickets."

Ellie's face brightened, and he had to admit, it was worth the cost of the tickets just to see it. So he reached into his pocket, pulled out a money clip and removed a hundred-dollar bill.

"How much are the tickets?" he asked one of the teens.

"Five dollars each."

"Then I'll take twenty."

While the teenager counted out the tickets, Steven turned to Ellie. "Are you going?"

"I wouldn't miss it."

Then neither would he.

"You won't be sorry," Ellie said as he pocketed

the tickets. "Some of those kids are incredibly talented. I really enjoyed it last year."

Steven had planned to give away the tickets he'd just purchased, but maybe he ought to actually attend, especially if it would help him get on the mayor's good side.

As they strolled through the open-air marketplace, Steven and Dillon were met with more than a few wary stares. One guy wearing a red plaid shirt and a pair of denim overalls narrowed his eyes and studied them suspiciously. The obvious distrust in the older man's gaze didn't seem to bother Dillon, but it troubled Steven—probably more than it should.

Back in Fort Lauderdale, the Fortune family had a stellar reputation. Their father had made millions by getting in on the ground floor of the video game industry. And after he married Steven's mother, Marci, the couple soon got involved in several charities and philanthropic projects that had benefited the entire city. People appreciated them there.

But that wasn't the case here in Rambling Rose, and Steven found the locals' animosity unsettling and bothersome.

When David Fortune married Marci, he'd had two sons of his own, Callum and Dillon. Soon after, he adopted her sons, Steven and his younger brother Wiley. The couple then went on to have four daughters together.

Ever since he was a boy, Steven had been proud of the family name and had tried his best to prove himself worthy of it. His father might have treated all of his children the same, but Steven couldn't seem to forget that he wasn't a Fortune by blood. But that didn't make him any less loyal.

Ellie strode toward the scowling older man and reached out her hand to greet him. "How's it going, Frank? Did you and Helen take that trip to Oklahoma last weekend to visit the kids?"

"We sure did." Frank's expression morphed from suspicion to outright pride and joy. "We drove up there last Friday. And on Saturday afternoon, we got to see Billy play basketball. I have to tell you, Ellie. That boy isn't too tall, but he's got a good eye and quick hands. He's fast on his feet, too, and he's becoming a dang good player. I hate to brag, but it wouldn't surprise me if the college scouts got wind of him and started banging on his door before the end of the season."

"That's awesome, Frank. I don't blame you for being a proud grandpa." Ellie turned to Steven and Dillon. "Frank, have you met Dillon and Steven Fortune yet?"

A slight scowl returned to the older man's face. "Can't say I have."

"They're eager to meet some of the people

who've lived in town for years," she said. "They'd like to get your take on their plans to open that new hotel."

Frank waited a couple of beats, then extended his arm and greeted each brother with a work-roughened hand. "I won't pull any punches. Most of us don't like the idea of that hotel one little bit."

"What don't you like about it?" Steven asked.

Frank chuffed. "It's too damned big and fancy for a town like Rambling Rose." He studied Steven for a beat, then folded his arms across his chest. "I suspect that's why you boys are having trouble getting the planning commission's approval."

That was true. The commission seemed to be split right down the middle, with very little sign of yielding.

"They have a few concerns," Steven admitted, "and we're trying to work them out."

"No surprise there," Frank said. "If you ask me—and practically everyone else you'll find here at Mariana's Market—you'd be a heck of a lot more successful if you were building a motel instead of a five-star hotel, although some folks are opposed to any additional lodging in town that would attract more tourists."

Yeah. Right. There was no way Steven or his brothers would even consider downsizing to a motel. But he didn't want to stir up trouble before they'd taken more than ten steps into the market.

"Thanks for the suggestion, Frank. I'll keep that in mind."

"We'd best be moving along," Ellie said. "Give Helen my best."

Once they'd gotten out of earshot, Dillon let out a soft whistle, followed by a half chuckle and an elbow nudge. "You're going to think about it, huh? There's no way you or Callum would agree to a project like that."

Steven shot his brother a look meant to suggest he should keep his mouth shut. He was making some headway with Ellie and didn't want to risk losing what little they'd gained. Besides, the longtime Rambling Rose residents might not trust the Fortunes or any other newcomers, but it didn't take long for Steven to realize they adored their young mayor.

Up ahead, a middle-aged man wearing a straw hat with a torn brim and a green apron stood behind a produce stand. When the ruddy-cheeked fellow spotted Ellie, he called out, "Good morning, Mayor. I got some of those sweet strawberries you like. They go pretty fast, so I put a couple of boxes under my table for you."

Ellie brightened, and while her smile was directed at the produce vendor, just seeing it turned Steven's heart on end. "Thank you, Pete. I'll come back to get them before I leave. And I'd like some of your broccoli, too."

"You got it!"

As they made their way through the market, Dillon asked, "So who's Mariana? What's her claim to fame?"

"She has a food truck in the center of the market. It's been there for years, but over time, as she and her menu gained popularity, other people who had stuff to sell began showing up. And that's how this became known as Mariana's Market."

"Sounds like an interesting beginning to an unusual business," Steven said.

"Yes, and it's a little mysterious, too. Even though she's been around for ages and is loved and well-known in the community, I don't think Mariana is her given name. She's a bit of an enigma, especially when it comes to her roots. When she and her mother first acquired that food truck, it had *Mariana's* painted on the side. So she took on the moniker herself for promotional purposes. Since she never talks about her past, some of the locals think she had a personal reason for a name change. No one knows for sure, and she won't confirm anything. So people keep guessing."

"She sounds like an intriguing character," Steven said. "I'd like to meet her."

"You will." Ellie tossed him a bright-eyed smile that turned him inside out. "A trip to Mariana's Market wouldn't be the same without stopping by and ordering one of her meat-loaf sandwiches or the chicken fried steak and potato salad."

"So she specializes in down-home cooking," Steven said.

"For the most part. She also includes a couple of southwestern specialties on her menu, which vary. But on the weekends, she always has menudo. People claim she makes the best in town, but I'd have to disagree. When it comes to Mexican food, Alma Hernandez—my mother—is the best cook in all of Texas. But don't tell Mariana."

"Menudo?" Dillon scrunched his brow. "Is that the spicy soup made out of tripe? If so, I think I'll pass."

Ellie gave Steven a playful nudge with her arm, as if they'd become friends. "What about you? Are you braver and more adventurous than your brother?"

"I don't know about that," Steven replied. "Dillon's not afraid of much. But if you say it's good, I'll give it a try."

As they ventured on, Ellie stopped to introduce Steven and Dillon to some of the vendors and several shoppers. As long as the brothers had the pretty young mayor to vouch for them, most of the people seemed to accept them.

Next up was a group of senior citizens who met every Saturday morning at the community center and caught a shuttle van to the market. Some came looking for knickknacks or arts and crafts, but most seemed to consider the outing a social event.

Steven had to admit he'd met a lot of colorful but likable characters, but none of them was likely to venture to the Shoppes to purchase a bespoke suit, a Louis Vuitton purse or gourmet vegan cuisine. And when asked, not a one was in favor of the hotel development.

No wonder the planning commission had been giving Fortune Brothers Construction such a hard time. But Steven wasn't one to shy from a fight.

They paused when they came upon a card table with four older men playing gin rummy.

An older man with a head of thick white hair looked up from his cards with a smug grin. "Well, I'll be damned. Would you look at this?"

"Oh, for cripe's sake." A balding fellow sitting next to him furrowed his brow. "Don't give me that, Cotton Head. You can't possibly have gin now. I just dealt the cards."

Another guy said, "Norm, you didn't shuffle them very good, so if he does, I wouldn't be surprised."

"Oh yeah?" Norm let out a snort. "Cotton Head, if you can call gin now, I'll give you two hours to gather a crowd in town square, then I'll kiss your ass."

Cotton Head offered up a big gap-toothed grin,

laid down his hand and said, "Then you'd better pucker up, Norm."

At that, Dillon let out a laugh. A bright smile, once a familiar sight Steven hadn't seen in a while, stretched across his face and glimmered in his eyes. "Those guys are a hoot."

"Aren't they?" Ellie lowered her voice. "And you haven't seen anything yet. But they're more than a couple of funny old men hanging out at a flea market and poking fun at each other. They're actually veterans who do a lot for the town. In fact, twice a week, they drive out to Austin and volunteer at a soup kitchen. They don't just dish out plates of food and pat themselves on the back for doing a good deed. They actually sit down and eat at the tables, talking to people and treating them like old friends."

"Do you think they'd mind if I watched for a while?" Dillon asked Ellie.

"No, not at all. They always draw a crowd and seem to like it."

As Dillon lingered behind, Steven and Ellie continued to walk through the market.

"It's good to hear my brother laugh," Steven said. "He's been pretty quiet and low-key ever since we moved here."

"Sounds to me as if your brother misses his life in Florida."

"Maybe so. But he's a big part of Fortune Brothers. And he's adjusting."

Ellie's pace slowed as she approached a weathered brown-and-white motor home with an outstretched blue canopy. Various pieces of antique furniture had been placed in front of it, while a rectangular table displayed smaller items for sale.

"I love antiques," Ellie said. "And my mom collects old jewelry. Do you mind if I look around for a minute or two?"

"Not at all. Take your time."

As Ellie picked up an elaborate necklace with blue, green and purple stones set in a peacock design, Steven made his way to the left of her to look at a couple of old books and magazines that rested at the edge of the table.

He spotted a fragile brown copy of *The Poetical Works of Sir Walter Scott* that had to be more than a hundred and fifty years old. He was about to pick it up when a faded red scrapbook caught his eye. He opened it instead. "Wow."

"What did you find?" Ellie asked.

"This." He pointed to the old newspaper clippings someone had carefully glued inside. "It's a bunch of articles about Rambling Rose. Some of them date back to the early 1900s."

He carefully paged through it. "I can't believe this, Ellie. There's even a feature about Fortune's Foundling Hospital."

"That's awesome."

"I'm going to buy it." He glanced over his shoulder and motioned to the dark-haired vendor. "How much do you want for this?"

She shrugged. "Twenty dollars?"

He might have haggled, just for the fun of it, but he was too intent upon owning the scrapbook and taking his time to catch up on more of Rambling Rose's history.

Moments after they'd purchased both the peacock necklace and the scrapbook, Ellie said, "Should we head over to Mariana's now or wait for Dillon?"

"I can go back and tell him we're ready to eat."

In all honesty, though, Steven preferred to have more time with Ellie on his own, without his brother or the business or the family name to get in the way. He liked having the chance to get to know her better—not as the mayor, but as a young woman the town loved and admired.

Ellie might think that she was just like her neighbors, but there was more to her than that. A lot more. Something seemed to be happening between them, and while he wasn't sure what it was, it went beyond politics and business deadlines.

She'd shown him a side of the town she'd grown up in, and he wanted to introduce her to his world, too.

As they walked back to the card game, her

shoulder brushed against his arm, and he felt the strangest compulsion to take a hold of her hand, which would have been totally inappropriate. And stupid. But for some crazy reason, he felt more and more drawn to Ellie Hernandez as a person.

And worse, he was tempted to act on it before the day was done.

After taking Dillon away from his VIP seat at the weekly gin rummy game, Ellie led the two Fortune brothers to the center of the marketplace, where Mariana's food truck was parked. It was quite the experience, she supposed—being flanked by two gorgeous hunks, both muscular and at least six feet tall. They also had the same blue eye color, with only slight variations in the shade.

But there were more than a few subtle differences. Dillon's dirty-blond locks were slightly tousled, while Steven's dark, short-cropped hair was often covered by the black Stetson that seemed to have become a part of him since he'd moved to Texas.

Several times over the past hour or so, when the brothers weren't looking, Ellie had stolen a peek at them, just to check them out. Surprisingly, she hadn't been able to spot a family resemblance. Not that it mattered, she supposed. Some siblings took after different relatives.

Still, they were both eye candy in their own

right. And she hadn't been the only one checking them out, either. The brothers had caught the attention of just about every woman shopping at Mariana's Market today, drawing smiles from most of them. But it was Steven who'd captured Ellie's interest—and not just because of his sexy swagger, his damn good looks or the way those fancy jeans molded to his butt.

No, there was more to Steven Fortune that Ellie found appealing. His charm, she supposed. He also exuded confidence without any sign of pride or arrogance. And he was bright, too. Whenever she challenged him, he held his own.

Unlike a lot of men Ellie knew, Steven wasn't intimidated by her brains and political success. She had to admit that she found it refreshing.

Unable to help herself, she stole another glance at him, only to find him gazing at her in a way that set off a dizzying flutter in her chest. For a couple of beats, something stirred between them, and even though they continued to move through the crowd, the marketplace seemed to stand still.

Oh, for Pete's sake, Ellie. You didn't read any romantic interest in his eyes.

And even if she had, she'd better get over it. In a few short months, she'd be a mother with her hands full. It was going to be tough enough for her to put her baby boy first while trying to handle her job as mayor. So she'd be absolutely crazy to consider a romantic relationship—and a complicated one like this one would no doubt be. Her day planner was full enough as it was.

Besides, if Steven actually had dating on his mind, a rich, handsome man like him would run for the hills as soon as he learned she was pregnant.

Ellie shook off the foolhardy thought and pointed ahead at the food truck, where several people had already begun to fill the seats at the folding picnic tables set up out front. The red, black and white vehicle with chrome trim had gotten a fresh coat of paint since the last time she'd been here, as had the green swirly letters on the side that spelled out *Mariana's* in a fancy cursive font.

She pointed ahead. "There it is. We'd better place our orders while we can find a place to sit."

"Something sure smells good." Steven took a second whiff. "All of a sudden, I'm starving."

"I agree," Dillon said.

Mariana, a matronly woman with ruddy cheeks, warm brown eyes and bleached blond hair pulled into a bun, popped her head out the open window where she took orders and passed out food. She gave Ellie a little wave, then, in a graveled voice that was loud even when she whispered, she yelled, "Fred Willingham! Your meat-loaf sandwich is ready."

"That has to be Mariana," Steven said to Ellie.

"You've got that right."

As they got within five feet of the food truck, Fred said something to Mariana as he picked up his meal. The tall, slender man usually spoke in a soft tone, so Ellie couldn't hear what he said, but it must have been funny, because Mariana let out a raucous laugh.

Before Ellie had a chance to say hello to Fred, he turned to the left and walked away holding a foil-covered paper plate. But the matronly woman remained at the open window and broke into a big ol' grin. "Howdy, Mayor. What do you think of the new paint job?"

"It looks good." Ellie glanced at each of the brothers, then back to Mariana. "I'd like to introduce you to Steven and Dillon Fortune."

"Well, now." Mariana crossed her arms and eyed both men carefully. "This is a surprise. You fellows have been the talk of the town, and I don't mean just among the gossipmongers. But I gotta say, you two don't look like rich vermin to me."

"Actually," Steven said, offering her a charming smile, "my brothers and I are pretty harmless."

"Good to know. But just in case one of you should get a wild hair, I keep a shotgun near the cash register, and I know how to use it." Mariana waited a beat, then winked at the men, who hadn't quite figured out how to take her, and let out another hearty laugh.

"I've been telling them about the locals," Ellie told Mariana. "About the people who've called Rambling Rose home for years. It's hard for them to understand that we're simple folk with big hearts and a strong work ethic. So I brought them to the marketplace so they could see for themselves just how special this town really is."

Mariana arched a brow and studied the men. "So now you're here. What do you think of us?"

"You're all pretty colorful and likable, especially Norm and the boys playing gin rummy." Steven cracked a grin and nodded his head toward Dillon. "I was afraid my brother was going to sit down and join the game."

"They'd welcome a newbie like you," Mariana said, "but if you take 'em up on it, you'd better hold on to your wallet. Losing to those guys won't be cheap."

"I'll keep that in mind," Dillon said.

"So what'll it be?" Mariana asked. "I've got meat loaf and fried chicken on the menu today. And the southwestern special is green chili and homemade tortillas."

"How about the menudo?" Ellie asked.

"Sorry. I'm afraid you're out of luck. I got off to a slow start this morning and didn't get a chance to cook up a new batch."

"That's too bad." Steven winked and jabbed an elbow at Dillon's arm. "My brother and I had our hearts set on having a great big bowl of it."

"If you come back next weekend, I'll have it for sure. And your first bowl is on the house." Mariana glanced at Ellie. "You guys gonna eat? Or did you just stop by to hold up the food line?"

Ellie couldn't help but laugh. "I'll have the fried chicken."

"Me, too," Steven added.

Dillon said, "Make that three."

Twenty minutes later, after they'd eaten their fill of some of the best fried chicken and homemade potato salad in Texas, they called it a day and returned to the car.

As Dillon climbed into the back seat, Ellie paused before opening the driver's door. She probably could've waited to question the brothers until the drive back to town, but Dillon hadn't done much talking today. And she couldn't quell her growing curiosity.

"So what did you think?" she asked Steven.

"About what?" A crooked smile tweaked one side of his lips and dimpled his right cheek. "The people we met here?"

She nodded.

"I'll admit, it's been eye-opening. Up until a couple of days ago, when we had that run-in with the protesters at the grand opening of the Shoppes, I had no idea how much local resistance we were facing."

Ellie's hands hung at her sides, and she fought the urge to cross her fingers. "Does that mean you'll reconsider your plans to build that big luxury hotel?"

"Not really. You and the people who frequent Mariana's Market might not like it, but the newcomers in town will welcome a nice place for their friends and family to stay while visiting. On the other hand, the tour has given me a lot to think about and consider. So thank you for bringing us here today."

"You're welcome. Were you surprised to see this side of Rambling Rose?"

"Yes, but I saw something else that I hadn't expected to see. And that's making me reconsider a lot of things."

"Like what?" she asked, wanting to hear him out.

He scanned her from head to toe and back again, his gaze practically caressing her. Then he offered her a smile.

Her cheeks warmed, and she wondered what he was getting at. And what that appreciative grin meant. Instead, she pushed for a different response. "Aren't you going to answer my question? What did you see that gave you pause?"

"I saw the way you relate to the people—and

vice versa. They love and respect you as much as you love and respect them."

"There's a reason for that. I haven't lived in Rambling Rose my entire life. I was adopted when I was six. But it wasn't just my parents who took in a scared, awkward little girl in pigtails. Everyone in town adopted me, too. So I consider them all part of my family."

"You're lucky."

"Don't I know it."

Sometimes it seemed as if Ellie had grown up as a princess in a fairy-tale life. Once upon a time, she'd been a neglected, frightened and malnourished little girl who'd been rescued from a crack house by a king and queen who weren't able to have children of their own. And she'd never forgotten that. So for that reason, she'd spent the last twenty-two years trying to make her adoptive parents proud and to prove to them, as well as the entire community, that they'd made a wise choice in accepting her as one of their own. And for that reason alone, she dreaded having to tell them that she was about to be an unwed mother.

But that was way too much to share with anyone, especially one of the new, rich residents.

"The Rambling Rose locals trust me," she said. "Not a day goes by that I don't know that, that I don't respect it. And I feel the weight of that trust every day."

He nodded and smiled. "I'm sure you do."

She inadvertently placed a hand on her tummy and stopped short of giving it a loving caress. What had been a small bulge last week was developing into an actual baby bump, which meant her secret would be out soon enough. It was time to tell her parents. And then she'd have to make an announcement to the community.

Maybe it would be in her best interest to tell Steven first. She could practice her confession on him, and once she'd done that, she wouldn't be able to drag her feet any longer on telling the people she loved.

Actually, that would solve another mounting problem. Once she'd told Steven she was pregnant, neither of them would waste another minute thinking about wacky romantic ideas.

Satisfied with her new game plan, she turned toward the driver's door.

"How about having dinner with me tonight?" Steven asked.

Even though she'd half expected him to ask a question like that, her lips parted, and she slowly turned back to face him. "I…uh… Thank you, but I don't think that's a good idea."

"Why not?"

She glanced to her right and then to her left. Several other people had followed them out to the parking lot.

"I don't want to explain in public," she said. "I'll tell you when we're alone."

"Then a private dinner it is." He tossed her a boyish grin. "How about tonight, at the Fame and Fortune Ranch?"

Chapter Four

The drive back to town seemed to take a lot longer than the ride out to Mariana's Market. It was a lot quieter, too. If Ellie hadn't been nearly drowning in remorse for accepting Steven's dinner invitation, she might have tried to break the awkward silence.

Steven had assured her that the Fame and Fortune Ranch was the best place for them to speak confidentially, but the more she thought about the logistics, the more she doubted his claim. After all, his entire family lived on the property. Well, at least those who'd moved to Rambling Rose from Fort Lauderdale.

She'd heard through the grapevine that the fancy-schmancy house was laid out in a way that provided them all with a certain amount of privacy, but she found that hard to believe. And what about household help? Maids, butlers and cooks—oh my!

By the time she reached the city limits, she decided to ask him for a rain check—one she'd never use.

Since Dillon hadn't been privy to Steven's invitation, she wouldn't mention it until after she dropped off the brothers at their pickup. Then she'd take Steven aside and tell him she'd just remembered her plans to go out with her friend Daria this evening, so she'd have to pass.

But by the time they arrived at city hall, she'd changed her mind yet again. Everyone in Rambling Rose had been talking about the Fortunes' renovated, ranch-style home. From what she'd heard, the sprawling estate would boggle the mind of a common person. So Ellie actually would like to see it. On top of that, it might be a good idea—politically speaking, of course—for her to interact with Steven and his family on their own turf. Then, after dinner, she'd ask him to walk her out to her car. That's when she'd tell him about the baby.

Granted, it would be a difficult conversation to have, a rather embarrassing one. But once she'd gotten that out of the way, she'd go to her parents' house and give them the news.

Eventually, the community would learn her secret, too. At that point, she'd deal with any repercussions that might arise.

One day at a time, she told herself, *one good deed after another.* That had been her mantra for as long as she could remember, and it had led her to becoming a perfectionist, an overachiever and a leader.

Only trouble was, Ellie wasn't perfect. Deep down, she felt like an impostor. And now everyone in Rambling Rose would know it.

The whispers would eventually die down, she supposed, and everything would fall into place. Then she'd finally be able to openly celebrate the upcoming birth of her baby. Her son. A tiny human being who'd need her to look after him, to encourage him and to love him with all her heart.

When she stopped next to the pickup to let both Fortune brothers out of her car, she told them goodbye.

Dillon got out of the car first and shut the passenger door, but Steven remained seated beside her, holding the brown paper sack that held the old scrapbook he'd purchased and looking at her. A slow smile stretched across his gorgeous face. "I'll see you later."

Still, he didn't reach for the door. His eyes lingered on her for a beat. As their gazes locked, her breath caught, and her pulse kicked up a notch.

"Does six o'clock work for you?" he asked.

For some reason, the words jammed up in her throat, making it impossible to utter a sound, so she nodded her agreement.

"Great." Then he got out of the car.

Once the passenger door snapped shut, Ellie didn't wait for him to get into his own vehicle. Instead, she drove off, hoping she hadn't made another big mistake. But they seemed to be tiptoeing around attraction, pondering whether to act upon it. And that needed to stop.

Once Steven knew she was pregnant, her life would take a slow turn to normal. The flirtatious smiles, as well as her heart flips and flutters, would soon be a thing of the past.

Minutes later, she turned down Pumpernickel Court, a small subdivision that was built near the elementary school in the 1960s. She pulled into the driveway. Using the remote on her sun visor, she opened the garage door and parked next to Daria's late-model Prius.

Three months ago, Daria had been working for an accounting firm in Austin, but the company downsized and she was let go. Knowing Daria, she would've taken the layoff in stride, calling it a little inconvenience. But she'd just gone through a major breakup, so it hadn't taken much to knock her off balance. She'd called Ellie that evening in tears.

"Rent a U-Haul trailer," Ellie had said. "Then pack up your stuff and come to Rambling Rose. I've got a spare bedroom, and it's yours for as long as you need it."

Two days later, Daria arrived. The timing had worked perfectly. Ellie and Mike had recently split, so the two new roommates had shared their disappointment and pain caused by men who were all hat and no cattle. And now the roomies were relieved and glad to be single.

Ellie closed the garage door and entered the house through the outdated kitchen.

"I'm home," she called out as she set her purse on the kitchen counter.

Tank bounded toward her, greeting her with a happy whimper and a wagging tail. He miscalculated his speed and tried to slow his pace, but he tripped over his big paws and tumbled to a stop at her feet.

"You silly guy. What're we going to do with you?" Ellie gave him a scratch behind his floppy ears.

"Hey," Daria said from the doorway. "You're home."

"Yep." Ellie straightened but continued to study the rascally pup. "I swear Tank has doubled in size in the past couple of weeks. The lease allows us to have one small pet, but that puppy is going to outgrow anyone's definition of 'small' before we know it. The landlords are going to freak when they see him."

"You're probably right." Daria crossed the kitchen, opened up the pantry, removed a dog biscuit from the box and handed it to Tank.

Ellie scanned the floral wallpaper, yellowed and faded from age, the pink Formica countertops, and outdated white appliances. The entire house could have used a major renovation decades ago, but the owners hadn't wanted to spend the money.

Even though the house was a rental, Ellie planned to buy new blinds and paint the third bedroom and turn it into a nursery.

"If the landlord doesn't want Tank here," Daria said, "I'll have to look for a new place."

That might sound like an easy solution, but Daria's part-time job as a bookkeeper at the car wash didn't pay much, so she wouldn't be able to afford a dog-friendly place until she found a better position.

"How's the housebreaking coming along?" Ellie asked.

"Awesome. Tank's doing great. He hasn't had an accident all day. Every time I take him outside, he goes potty."

"Sounds like you're the one who's being trained."

Daria laughed. "Yeah, you're right."

If the landlord did complain about Tank, Ellie

and Daria might have to house hunt together. They'd both gotten attached to the rascally pup. He was a little goofy but lovable. He was also a little troublesome. "Did he chew up anything today?"

"Nothing but his toys. But then, I've been following him around like a coyote circling a chicken coop."

"That's good to hear. I don't want to lose another pair of heels."

"Sorry about that." Daria reached for another dog biscuit and handed it to Tank.

As she did, Ellie took a moment to watch her friend, who was the prettiest woman she'd ever known. Daria's biracial father had been in the military and stationed in Hawaii when he met and married her mother, who was a Pacific Islander. Daria seemed to have inherited all the best qualities of every race and culture represented on her family tree, including long dark curly hair, blue-green eyes and tanned skin. The men in town had noticed, too, but Daria claimed she wasn't interested in dipping her toes back in the dating pool.

After giving Tank a pat on the head, Daria straightened and brushed her hands against her slacks. "So, how'd the tour of Mariana's Market go?"

"Okay, I guess. But I don't think the Fortune brothers will alter their plans for that fancy hotel. So I'm not sure how helpful it was in the long run."

"By the way," Daria said, "I took some chicken out of the freezer. I thought I'd add some barbecue sauce and bake it. How's that sound?"

Ellie took a deep breath, then slowly let it out. "It sounds good, but I'm not eating at home tonight."

"You have another meeting? On Saturday night?"

"Sort of. I'm having dinner with Steven at the Fame and Fortune Ranch."

Daria's jaw dropped. "No kidding? Does he know about...?"

"The baby? Not yet. So far, you're the only one I've told. But I'm going to let him know tonight."

Daria leaned against the kitchen counter and crossed her arms. "Before you tell your mom and dad?"

"That's my plan. He seems to be interested in me—romantically. So tonight, when we're alone, I'll tell him I'm pregnant. That ought to cool his heels. And it'll force me to quit dragging my feet and finally face my parents with the news."

Daria let out a little whistle. "You might want to rethink that."

"Telling my parents?"

"No. You *need* to do that. And sooner rather than later. But it just seems weird to share that news with Steven first." Daria eyed Ellie carefully, then blew out a slow whistle. "OMG. He's not the only one having a few romantic thoughts, is he?"

Ellie might have waved her off, told her she was wrong. But Daria knew her almost as well as she knew herself. "All right. I find him attractive. But even if he were interested in dating a pregnant woman—and I'm one hundred percent sure he wouldn't be!—I'd never go out with him. We have too many opposing ideas."

"I've always believed the old adage that opposites attract."

"Maybe. But they don't make for lasting relationships. We both learned that the hard way." Ellie nodded toward the doorway. "Come on. Let's go into the living room. I've been walking all over Mariana's Market, and I want to get off my feet."

As Daria followed her out of the kitchen with Tank on their heels, Ellie added, "On top of that, what would the community say if they thought I'd gone to the dark side?"

"Seriously?" Daria laughed. "You see Steven Fortune as Lord Vader? Come on, he's not that bad."

"Maybe not." Ellie plopped down in the brown recliner and kicked off her shoes. "But I'll have enough community disappointment to worry about within the next couple of days. I'm not going to throw a can of lighter fluid onto the flames.

Besides, I really need to focus on getting ready for the baby."

"I can't wait to help you. We'll have to plan several shopping trips. You're going to need a small dresser, a crib and some cute bedding. And once your parents find out, I'll bet your mom will want to convert one of their spare rooms into a nursery, too."

"True." There was no argument there. George and Alma Hernandez loved children, especially babies. They'd make awesome grandparents. "But it might take them a little while to get used to the idea. They're pretty conservative. I don't think they'll like me running around town barefoot and pregnant."

"Then wear your shoes." Daria smiled and slowly shook her head. "Come on, Ellie. You've never been an embarrassment to them. And you won't be now."

"I hope you're right. It's just that…"

"Your parents *adore* you. They'll get over any disappointment they may feel real quick. And in this day and age, that should take all of five minutes."

"You've got a point. It's just…" Ellie didn't keep much from Daria, but she'd never told anyone about the conversation she'd overheard when she was only six. Maybe now was the time to share it. "A couple of weeks after they first took me in as a foster child, I stood outside the kitchen door and heard my father ask my mom if she was sure she wanted to go through with their plan to adopt me."

"You can't blame him for that. Adoption is a big step. It's only natural that a couple would talk it over and make sure they're on the same page."

"I know. But he said something else. He asked if she thought I might have inherited any bad genes from my biological parents. I didn't understand all the words he'd used, but I knew what he meant. My biological father was a gang member serving a life sentence. And my mom was a druggie who cared more about her next fix than she did me." Ellie took a deep, fortifying breath, then slowly let it out. "Papa was afraid that, even if they provided me with love and a solid upbringing, I could turn out to be just like my birth parents."

"But you didn't."

"I know." Ellie gave a little shrug, hoping her friend could piece it all together—the insecurity that still lingered inside, popping out every now and then, the fear of failure that sometimes dogged her.

"How did your mother respond to that?"

"She told him they'd just have to take it one day at a time."

"Apparently, those days went by without a hitch."

"Only because I made up my mind to prove to them that I wasn't a bad seed."

"You don't think your parents know that?" Daria asked.

Ellie's shoulders slumped. "Yes. But for the record, my birth mom was never married to my dad. And she used to entertain a lot of men, if you know what I mean."

"Come on, Ellie. So you had sex with Mike. When you realized the relationship wasn't working, you split up. That's what a smart woman does. Your parents can't blame you for that. Dang, girl. The guy's a freelance photographer whose new job requires him to fly from country to country on photo shoots. He'd never be around. And, on top of that, he didn't want kids. Ever."

"You're right. I'd hoped he'd change his mind in time, so I respected that. But then I got bronchitis, and the antibiotic must have made my birth control pills ineffective. We used a condom, but he wasn't happy about it and got a little careless."

Mike had been a bad choice from the get-go. And Ellie should have been smarter, should have picked up on his flaws earlier.

"Ditch the pity party," Daria said. "Let's focus on the upside. You're going to have a sweet baby boy, and I'm going to be a godmother and an honorary auntie."

Ellie blessed her friend with a smile. "He's going to be a lucky little boy, one who's well loved from the day he arrives."

"You got that right. That little peanut isn't going to want for anything."

Except a father.

Ellie rested her head against the backrest and closed her eyes as she recalled the day she'd told Mike she was pregnant.

"You gotta be kidding," he'd said.

"I'd never joke about something like this."

They'd already broken up for several reasons, his new job assignment for one, and she'd known he wouldn't be happy with the news.

"I'm not ready for a kid, Ellie. And you just got elected mayor. You don't need to be burdened with one now, either. How soon can you schedule an abortion?"

She'd cringed at the thought of the solution he'd suggested. The baby might be unplanned, but unlike her parents had done to her, she'd never put her needs and desires over those of her child.

"I won't take that route," she'd told him.

"Don't expect me to take that journey with you. I'm flying out to South America in two weeks."

And he'd done just that.

What would Steven think when she told *him* tonight? Not that it mattered. Mike hadn't had a problem walking away from his own flesh and blood. No way would a man, especially one as rich and handsome as Steven Fortune, want to deal with someone else's baby.

And Ellie had better not let another fruitless thought like that cross her mind again.

As Steven drove Dillon home, he made a mental list of what he'd need to do before Ellie arrived—and the top of that list was to figure out what kind of groceries to buy.

Manny, the family cook and ranch caretaker, was off this weekend, which was just as well. Steven preferred to prepare dinner for her in his private quarters.

"Hey," Dillon said, "aren't you listening to me?"

Had he said something? "Sorry, I was deep in thought."

"Me, too," Dillon said. "About the hotel. If the people we met today are a good representation of the community at large, we're going to have a hard time getting the project approved. Maybe we ought to scrap the original plan."

Steven shook off his thoughts about his date with Ellie and got back to business. "No way am I going to roll over. That hotel, as planned, will be good for the town as a whole. I'll just have to use a little more charm and finesse."

"With whom?" Dillon cut a glance across the seat and cracked a smile. "The planning commission? Or the beautiful mayor?"

Steven didn't respond.

"Cat got your tongue?" Dillon asked. "You can't deny it. I saw fireworks between the two of you today."

"They were probably one-sided."

"No, it went both ways. Ellie might consider you an opponent, but she's attracted to you, too."

Thoughts about Ellie always kicked up Steven's pulse a notch. He'd suspected that she felt something for him, but realizing that his brother had picked up on those vibes, too, validated his suspicion and sent his blood pumping.

Silence filled the cab as they neared the ranch, then Dillon spoke again. "Did you see the way she interacted with the people at Mariana's Market?"

"How could I miss it? She's like a rock star to them." In fact, Steven was a bit dazzled by her himself, not that he'd admit it. "It's not likely that she'll change her mind about the hotel. She still thinks it's too big, fancy and expensive for the common folk."

"Since when have you ever let a stubborn politician stop you?"

"Never." And Steven wasn't about to let one stop him now. He'd work on Ellie a little more at dinner. "By the way, Dillon, I hope you have plans tonight."

"Why's that?"

"I invited Ellie to come over."

"I knew it."

"You don't know squat. It's just a business meeting."

"The hell it is." Dillon chuckled. "You've got more than business on your mind, brother."

Maybe so. He had to admit he was eager to spend more time with her. But no matter how big the Fame and Fortune Ranch was, he wanted to entertain her in private. And since Callum and Becky were spending the night in Austin with the twins and Stephanie had recently fallen in love with Acton Donovan and was now living with him on his ranch, tonight was Steven's best chance of having Ellie to himself.

"Don't worry," Dillon said. "I'll make myself scarce. I've got a kitchen in my quarters, just like you do. So give it your best shot."

Four hours later, the doorbell rang, sparking a rush of excitement as Steven headed to the foyer. He'd already fired up the grill on his private patio. A couple of filets, seasoned just right, were waiting in the fridge, and he'd completed all the prep work for a salad.

He swung open the door, and while he'd known the pretty mayor would be standing on the stoop, he hadn't been prepared to see her looking so… amazing. Her glossy black hair hung loose and down her back, allowing him to see how long it actually was. Her brown eyes were larger and more luminous than usual, and a shy smile stretched across her pink-glossed lips.

"Come in," he said as he stepped aside and watched her enter the house rocking a pair of dark jeans and a funky T-shirt with a Rosie the Riveter print. The woman who looked hot in whatever she wore never ceased to surprise him.

He led her through the foyer, with its travertine flooring, floor-to-ceiling windows and Southwestern artwork, and to the east, toward his private quarters.

"You have a nice house," she said, her gaze taking in the decor. "Or should I say estate?"

"*House* works for me." He offered her a disarming smile. "We didn't all live together in Florida, but we got a good deal on this place. Another developer built it for himself and his fiancée. But the couple split up before they moved in, so Callum, Dillon and I snatched it up."

"Hmm. That seems to be your MO. You just pick up projects that were abandoned prior to completion."

"Can you blame us?"

"No, I suppose not." Ellie's steps slowed as she took a moment to scan the expansive living room that was rarely used. "It does seem like a luxurious mansion."

"I guess you're right. There are two guest houses and enough land for us to build more, if the need should arise."

"Not to mention the guard at the gate who let me in."

"The gatehouse is a new addition to the property." And only a precaution. The disgruntled people who'd formed protest groups were probably harmless, but Steven and his brothers decided a little extra security wouldn't hurt.

"I didn't expect the Fame and Fortune Ranch to be a luxurious compound."

"I prefer to call it a ranch. You'll have to check out the stable."

"I'm sure it's impressive," she said.

Right now, the only one he wanted to impress was her.

"So where is everyone?" she asked.

"It's just you and me tonight."

Her gaze zeroed in on his, setting off a flurry of pheromones that damn near took him out at the knees. Talk about fireworks. Dillon had been right. Those colorful sparks were going both ways.

He was half tempted to reach for her, to pull her into his arms, but it was too soon. And he wasn't about to push when they had the whole evening in front of them.

"I thought I'd grill a couple of steaks—filet mignon. But if you're not into red meat, we can have chicken or salmon."

"No, that's fine. Steak sounds good." Her head tilted slightly, and a playful glimmer lit her eyes.

"What's the matter?"

"It's just that I never pegged you for a chef."

"I'm not. But I can whip up a decent meal when I want to. My sisters, the triplets, are super foodies. That's why they're going to open Provisions, the restaurant we're building."

"I hope they have some business experience. Restaurants take a lot of work."

"Actually, Ashley, Megan, and Nicole have a lot of experience working in restaurants. They've been cooking, waiting tables and working front of the house since they were in high school. And Nicole might be self-taught, but she's worked her way up to sous chef. She knows what she's doing."

Ellie scrunched her brow in the cutest way, and her head cocked slightly to the side.

"I know what you're probably thinking," he said. "A lot of people find it surprising that a man who'd made a fortune in the video game industry would insist that his children get jobs once they turned sixteen. But my dad figured it would build character. And that working would keep us out of trouble."

"You're right. I find it surprising. But it's also an admirable philosophy."

"It didn't hurt any of us," Steven said. "It taught us how to work for someone else, a boss who wasn't a parent or relative. And then, once we turned twenty-one, he gifted each one of us with a sizable check, something to add to our coffers."

"A bonus, huh?"

"Yes. If I ever have kids, I'm going to make them get jobs, too. I mean, once they're old enough."

She seemed to ponder that for a beat, then asked, "When are the girls coming to Rambling Rose?"

"Soon. Now that Stephanie has moved out, they'll take over her quarters on the other side of the house."

"I'll look forward to meeting them. And to trying out the food at Provisions."

Since Ellie had made it clear she wasn't into glitz or glamour, Steven feigned mock surprise and placed a hand on his chest. "Seriously? You'd actually eat at an upscale restaurant?"

"Believe it or not, I'm a bit of a foodie myself, whether it's down-home cooking prepared in a food truck or a five-star French restaurant in the city."

Apparently, there was a lot more to Ellie Hernandez than he'd once thought. She wasn't just a small-town girl doing her best to dig in her heels when it came to change. She wasn't just beautiful and savvy. She also had a heart, not just for Rambling Rose, but for the people she considered her tribe.

The more Steven talked to her, away from city hall and grand openings, the more she intrigued him. And tonight he looked forward to learning a lot more about her on his private patio.

And under a new moon and a starlit sky.

Chapter Five

Ellie sat at a glass-top table on Steven's small private patio, settling into the romantic ambiance he'd created this evening. He'd thought of everything. Twinkly lights on the trees and shrubs in the surrounding yard. An outdoor heater to chase the chill from the evening air. A yellow rose in a bud vase placed in the center of the table set for two. An uncorked bottle of red wine. A crystal decanter of water.

There was no way he had the time to set a scene like this unless he'd used hired help. Of course, he certainly could afford it. In fact, an estate this large probably required a full staff, some of whom might even live on the premises.

But then again, an ultrarich, handsome bachelor like Steven might have created this secluded spot, with lights in the trees, for him to use as a permanent romantic prop for the women he brought home.

Even the night sky seemed to have fallen under his magical orchestration, as if he'd snapped his fingers to chase away the clouds and reveal a big yellow moon surrounded by a million shining stars.

When Steven walked through the open sliding glass door and dazzled her with a smile, Ellie darn near fell under his spell, too. He carried two crystal wine goblets and set them on the table. "I thought a zinfandel would go best with the filet mignon, but if you'd rather have white, there's a sauvignon blanc chilling in the fridge."

"Thank you, but I'd prefer water." She probably should have explained why she was avoiding alcohol. It would have been a good segue into her announcement. But she wasn't quite ready to drop the bomb on him.

Or maybe she just didn't want to see a curtain come crashing down on the magical scene.

Whatever the actual reason, she added, "I'm driving."

He nodded, filled her goblet with water then poured the zinfandel for himself.

Eager to change the subject to one that was safer

and more comfortable, she asked, "So how many brothers and sisters do you have? And which one is oldest?"

"There are eight of us. I'm the oldest."

She'd suspected as much. He seemed to have taken a leadership position within the family.

He took a seat across from her. His gorgeous eyes studied her so intensely that she could feel him watching her. For a moment, she wished things were different, that her life wasn't complicated. That he wasn't so good-looking, so charming… And even more than that, she wished she wasn't expecting another man's baby.

Steven lifted his goblet and, after giving the zinfandel a little swirl that tinted the glass, he took a sip. "I was three and Wiley was two when our mom met David Fortune. They fell in love, and when they got married, David adopted me and my brother. And our mom adopted Callum and Dillon. So we're a blended family. Then Stephanie and the triplets came along."

"Yours, mine and ours. That's nice."

"It is now. We've all grown to love and respect each other, but it wasn't that nice at first. Callum and I didn't hit it off. He was used to being the top dog in his family, and then I came along, usurped his position and became his big brother."

"I can see where there'd be problems blending

two families," she said, "but you're lucky to have siblings. I'm an only child."

"There were times I wished I'd been one, too. But eventually things changed, especially when we began to play sports in high school and worked together in construction. Admiration and respect grew, and now we're not only brothers but business partners."

"That's cool."

"I think so." Steven pushed back his chair. "If you'll excuse me, I'm going to put the steaks on."

A few minutes later, while the meat was grilling, he returned to the table. Instead of taking his seat, he placed a hand on her shoulder, setting off a spiral of heat. "So what about you, Ellie?"

What about her? What was she feeling? How did his gentle touch affect her? Where were her wayward thoughts going?

"What do you mean?"

His fingers trailed off her shoulder, and he stepped to the right and took his seat. "What was it like being an only child?"

Aw. A safe topic. She could handle that. "Actually, you and I have one thing in common. The circumstances were a lot different, but I was adopted, too."

She fingered the stem of the water goblet. She wouldn't reveal where she'd come from or how she'd ended up in foster care at the home of a hardworking mechanic and a devoted schoolteacher. Or that her new parents, an older, childless couple, had once questioned whether she was a bad seed or a blessing.

"But being adopted is the only thing we have in common," she added. "I didn't grow up in the lap of luxury. And my parents believed that doing well in school was the only job I needed."

He took another slow sip of wine, clearly enjoying the taste. "So what about your plans for the future?"

"There's not much to tell." Her cheeks warmed at the lie, and her mouth went dry. She lifted her glass and took a cool, refreshing drink.

The conversation stalled while Steven finished grilling the steaks. Then he returned to the house and brought out two green salads. As he set one in front of Ellie, she caught an alluring whiff of his woodland-scented aftershave that trailed away as he took his seat, leaving her in a dreamy fog.

As they began to eat, her conscience rose up like a finger with an acrylic nail, poking her chest, insisting that she tell him now. Yet a rebellious spirit rose up, which suggested there might be some genetics at play after all, and insisted that she wait a bit longer.

She'd planned to tell him after dinner, right before she went home. Why change it up now?

"I know you and your brothers are business partners," Ellie said. "Who's the boss?"

"We're pretty much equal. I ran the main part of the construction/development firm in Florida. Dillon's big on details, so he's always been the nuts and bolts guy. And Callum took on the expansion and remote projects. I'd been chomping at the bit to get into the commercial side, and Callum said I'd get that opportunity in Rambling Rose. So here I am."

"Yes. Turning out one project after another."

"True. But we didn't start from scratch. We bought half-completed projects, which is why we were able to finish them in record time. That's probably what bothers you. It looks as if we're making a lot of changes all at once."

"Maybe so."

As much as she hated to admit it, she found herself admiring Steven, not just the adopted little boy, the high school student who worked construction, but the man he'd become.

"Just so you know," Steven said, "Callum handled the pediatric center and I took a big interest in the veterinary clinic, since I'm a real animal lover."

"Did you have pets as a kid?"

"No. My mom was allergic to pet dander. We might have been able to have outdoor animals, but since she also had a lot of health issues, my dad refused to consider it."

"That's too bad. I had a dog named Sweetie Pie when I was a growing up. I think pets enrich a child's life."

"My sister Stephanie loves animals, too. She became a vet assistant back in Florida and has the same job here in Texas. She also has a houseful of pets, including a rabbit and Acton's one-eyed cat."

"And you have a ranch and horses." No wonder Steven had morphed into a cowboy so easily.

"I enjoy riding in my free time, but I'm pretty busy." He took another sip of wine. "You may have figured this out already, but I'm the one taking charge of the hotel."

"And that's why you take any criticism of the blueprints personally."

"I try not to." Steven flashed a charming cowboy grin, then stood to clear the table.

Ellie scooted her chair back, intending to help with the cleanup.

"Don't get up," he said. "I've got this."

"Me, too." She offered him a smile of her own, then carried her dishes inside and to the small kitchen.

They worked well together and had the counters wiped down and the dishwasher running in short order.

"Ready for dessert?" he asked.

"I'm pretty full."

"Maybe something light? I have raspberry sorbet."

"Sounds good."

Moments later, he served them both. Instead of returning to the patio or finding a seat in the house, they stood at the counter and ate the sweet treat—a perfect ending to a filling meal.

As Ellie took the last bite of her sorbet, Steven said, "It's been a great evening. Thanks for driving out here tonight. But you still haven't told me what you were afraid to say in public."

Um. Yeah. That. How could it have slipped her mind?

Probably because she'd blocked it out so she could have one last hour to pretend there wasn't anything stopping her and Steven from becoming more than two people who clashed over ideas and goals. Only they didn't seem to be clashing now. They seemed to have become friends. And the possibility of becoming more than that lingered on the horizon.

"Did you forget what you wanted to tell me?"

No, she hadn't. But before she could find the words to speak, he reached out and cupped her jaw. His thumb stroked her cheek, caressing it and sending a shiver of excitement from her head to her toes.

Her lips parted, and her breath caught.

"Maybe this will jog your memory," he whispered.

His touch, his heated gaze jogged more than her memory. She ought to take a step back, but she was so caught up in the moment, the woodsy scent of his cologne, the blasted romantic mood that had been growing all evening, that she couldn't seem to think, let alone move.

Steven brushed his mouth across Ellie's, softly, tentatively. The cool, sweet taste of raspberry sorbet lingered on her lips, and he was dying for more.

She leaned into him for a moment, kissing him back, but before he could slip his arms around her and draw her close, she pulled her mouth away from him and stepped to the side.

"What's the matter?" he asked.

"I'm sorry. I…" She tucked a glossy strand of dark hair behind her ear, revealing a small diamond stud. "I didn't mean for that to happen."

"You don't owe me an apology. We didn't do anything wrong. Something's been building between us for quite a while. And I'd be surprised if you claimed you weren't feeling it, too."

"Yes, I've felt it. But kissing wasn't a good idea."

He tossed her what he hoped was a disarming smile. "It seemed like a good one to me."

She slowly shook her head and blew out a ragged breath.

He studied her carefully, waiting for a response. When she didn't explain, he said, "I don't often get my signals mixed, and you were giving off some I'm-interested vibes."

"You're right. I don't blame you for picking up on them. And acting on them. But…" She bit down on her bottom lip, clearly wrestling with whatever she had on her mind.

When she didn't continue, he pressed her to go on. "Is it because of our different backgrounds?" If so, that would be a new one for him. Most women fell all over themselves to date a rich and success-ful man.

"No," Ellie said. "That's not it."

Good. If his wealth didn't impress her, that made her all the more appealing to him.

"I hope you're not worried about our political dif-ferences," he said. "Or the potential conflict down at city hall. Because, believe it or not, you and I both want what's best for Rambling Rose."

"I'll admit that's a factor, but it's not the biggest one."

Then there was only one other reason. "Are you involved with someone else?"

"No. Not really. It's just…" She stood tall, sucked in a deep breath and blew out the words. "I'm pregnant."

Pregnant.

The word reverberated in the small kitchen, bouncing off the walls like the little ball in a pin-ball machine.

Wow. He hadn't seen that coming. He probably ought to respond, but he'd be damned if he knew what to say.

Congratulations?

Who's the lucky guy?

It sure as hell wasn't him.

And what was with her response to his question about there being someone else? *No. Not really?*

What the hell did that mean?

Steven might be dazed, even stupefied, but he couldn't very well just stand there. He had to say something. "I didn't realize… I mean, I might catch a lot of buzz from the Rambling Rose grapevine, but no one ever indicated you were…involved. Or dating."

"I try to be discreet when it comes to my private life. I dated a guy for quite a while, but we broke up about four months ago." She paused, clicked her tongue and closed her eyes.

Steven had no idea what to say. *I'm sorry?*

"And the guy…?" he asked.

She sucked in a deep breath, then slowly blew it out. "The relationship hadn't been working for either of us for a while, and I'm the one who finally called it quits. He knows about the baby, but he's not interested in being a father. In fact, he left the country."

From her frown and the twitch in her eye, he suspected she might not be happy about that.

"Are you sure you're over him?" Steven asked.

"Absolutely. His character flaws came out when I told him about the baby. I'm just sorry I didn't pick up on them earlier."

"So what's troubling you?"

"When the news gets out, and everyone finds out that I'm pregnant with no husband in sight…"

There'd be talk. That was for sure.

Ellie leaned a hip against the counter. "Things will probably get… Well, I'm not sure *ugly* is the right word, but it won't be cool." She looked at him, her eyes pleading. "Please keep that bit of news to yourself until I've made an announcement. My parents don't even know yet." She combed her fingers through her hair, mussing it in an oddly pretty way.

As he tried to sort through his thoughts, silence filled the room.

She studied him intently. Her brow furrowed, and her expression changed from one that was unbalanced to suspicious. "Steven, you're not going to say anything, are you?"

Hell, no. He could be trusted to keep a secret. And he wanted her to know that.

"No, of course not. I'm not one to…" *Kiss and tell* came to mind, but that wasn't how he'd meant to finish the dumbstruck statement. "Don't worry, Ellie. I won't say anything to anyone."

"Thank you." Then she turned and snatched

her purse from the kitchen chair, where she'd left it when she arrived. "I really need to go before it gets too late. I want to drive over to my parents' house and level with them."

"Okay. I'll walk you out."

"Good," she said. "I'd probably get lost trying to find the front door."

He lifted his hand to touch her back, to guide her down the hall, but thought better about it.

"Thanks for dinner," she said as they made their way through the house to the foyer.

"No problem."

But Ellie clearly had one. A big one. And for some dumb reason, which didn't make any sense at all, her problem now seemed to be his.

From the moment Ellie had driven away last night, Steven knew he'd screwed up. He should have said something to set things back on track. But that was the problem. He'd been completely stumped and speechless.

A barrage of emotion had been tumbling inside him ever since she'd told him she was pregnant— mostly surprise and frustration, followed by sympathy and a wallop of guilt.

Steven didn't get ruffled easily. No matter what the problem, he'd always been able to think himself out of a corner. But not this time. One wrong word, one wrong move on his part would have only made things worse.

His first thought was to avoid her until the news got out and then to wait until her world righted itself on its axis. But he'd never taken the coward's way out, and he wouldn't start now.

By the time Sunday morning rolled around and he'd had his first cup of coffee, he was no closer to a solution than he'd been before going to bed. So he decided to go to the stable and saddle Big Red. A long trail ride on his favorite horse usually helped clear his mind.

After pouring the remainder of his second cup of coffee into an insulated mug, he stepped out of one of the side doors into the yard, only to run into Dillon.

The minute his brother noticed him, a crooked grin broke across Dillon's face, and he crossed the yard, obviously wanting to talk. But Steven wasn't in the mood.

"So...?" Dillon asked. "How'd it go?"

"Fine."

Dillon's grin created a single dimple in his cheek. "Crashed and burned, huh?"

Steven wanted to smack what looked more like a smirk than a smile off his brother's face, which wasn't cool. Nor was it fair. Dillon had crashed and burned a few times himself.

Letting it go, Steven continued toward the stable. He had to get moving before everything began to close in on him.

"You going to saddle up Big Red?" Dillon asked.

"Yeah."

"You want to talk about it?"

"Nope. Ellie and I had a nice dinner. Then she went home."

"As simple as that?"

Steven shot him a frown. "Don't worry about it. Okay?"

Dillon lifted both hands as if in surrender, then took a dramatic step back, giving him a wide berth.

Good. He needed to have some time alone. He'd think about apologizing later.

The long trail ride seemed to help Big Red more than Steven. By the time he'd cooled down the horse and returned to the yard, Callum and Becky were climbing out of their car after their trip to Austin. The couple looked happy but exhausted.

Becky waved at Steven, then pressed her index finger to her lips, signaling him to be quiet right before she retrieved one sleeping twin from the car seat and Callum got the other.

Steven didn't mind being silenced. He didn't feel like talking to anyone right now anyway, especially about babies and outings to the zoo.

After Becky carried Luna into the house, Callum lingered, a sleeping Sasha in his arms, her head resting on his shoulder.

"How's it going?" Callum asked, his voice soft and low.

"Okay," Steven whispered.

"Don't worry about waking this one." Callum grinned. "Once Sasha's asleep, she's out."

"Did you guys have a good trip?" Steven asked, doing his best to appear remotely interested. "You look worn-out."

"I'm beat. But we had a lot of fun. It was a great trip. The kids slept all the way home."

"Good." Steven turned toward the house, eager to slip into his private living quarters.

"Hey," Callum called to his back.

Steven looked over his shoulder. "What?"

"Something's bothering you. What's up?"

"Nothing."

Callum furrowed his brow. "Like hell. Is there something going on I ought to know about?"

"Nope."

"I don't believe you."

Steven never had kept too many secrets from his brothers, especially Callum, who was good at reading him. "I've got stuff on my mind, but it's not business related, if that's what you're thinking. And it's no big deal. I spent some time riding Big Red, and now I've got it figured out."

Callum nodded as if he believed him.

Steven wished it were true. But he was a far cry from figuring anything out, and his foul mood continued to dog him all night long.

On Monday morning, it followed him to the Paz construction site, where they'd moved their modular office. Even his employees noticed, but most of them knew better than to approach him.

Fortunately, by the time he got home and turned in for the night, he'd finally realized what was actually bothering him, which led to a partial solution.

He couldn't stay away from Ellie any longer. Hell, he didn't want to. They were friends, even if that's as far as it would go. And she deserved more from him than he'd given her. Once he wrapped his mind around that, his mood lightened.

First thing tomorrow morning, he'd stop by the mayor's office bearing gifts and an apology that was long overdue.

Chapter Six

Ellie, who almost never cried, had bawled her eyes out all the way home from the Fame and Fortune Ranch.

"I can't believe how stupid I was," she'd told Daria when she got home. "I actually thought I could practice on Steven before telling my parents."

"How'd that work?" Daria asked.

Ellie pointed to her watery eyes, puffy from tears. "I couldn't walk into their house looking like this. They'd never believe that I have things under control."

"And what about the attraction? Did telling Steven stifle it?"

"You can say that again." Ellie rolled her eyes and plopped down on the recliner. "It certainly dashed Steven's feelings for me."

"But not yours for him?"

"Oh snap, Daria. I have no idea how I feel." She raked a hand through her hair. "I take that back. I feel stupid. It's got to be the pregnancy hormones. They've completely chased off my common sense."

"Did you kiss him?"

"Not really. I mean, he sort of kissed me. Briefly. It was sweet and tentative, but it wasn't a real one." Ellie let out whoosh of air and sat back in the chair.

"Ellie," Daria said, "if his lips lingered on yours for a couple of heartbeats, it was a kiss. Maybe not a let's-get-naked one. But he kissed you. And no matter how long it lasted, you liked it."

Yes, that was true. It would have been an amazing kiss—if she hadn't bolted. But she had. And she'd blasted him with the news of her pregnancy, shocking him senseless and chasing any and all lingering pheromones completely out of his breathing range.

And then she'd left in a rush, nearly tripping over her own feet.

For the rest of the weekend, guilt and embarrassment had hovered over her like a dark cloud ready to release a flood of rain on her at any moment.

Could she have botched things any worse?

Finally, on Monday, a bell-ringing thought struck. What about Steven? It's not like he was a victim in all of this. Ellie's revelation might have shocked him, but for a man who always had a charming smile and a ready response, he'd been dumbstruck. And when he did speak, he could have been a little more understanding and a lot kinder.

Even after shifting the blame onto Steven, she slept like crap again, and on Tuesday morning, she woke up tired and out of sorts. So she put off a visit to her mom and dad yet again. She'd made a mistake by dating Mike in the first place and would own up to it. But she wanted to assure her parents that she was happy about the baby and that she had a game plan for the future.

After she showered and blow-dried her hair, she used a little extra makeup, especially concealer under her eyes to hide the darkened, puffy bags. Then she dressed in a pair of black slacks, pulling the zipper up but leaving the top button undone. She chose a loose-fitting blouse and topped it off with a colorful scarf that would draw the eye to her face instead of her waistline.

She'd no more than entered the city hall lobby, her flats clicking against the Spanish tile flooring, when she spotted Steven standing near the water fountain holding a bouquet of yellow roses in one hand and a large pink box in the other. And wouldn't you know it? He looked just as gorgeous as ever.

What was he doing here?

His sheepish gaze, which seemed to look into the heart of her, suggested he'd come to see her. As he crossed the floor to approach her, any doubt faded.

"I brought you something," he said, handing her the flowers.

She raised the palm of her hand to stop him. "I'm not allowed to accept gifts from anyone."

"Even flowers?"

"I don't want anyone to think I'm taking a bribe."

Steven's lips quirked into a playful grin. "Do you always play that strictly by the rules?"

"Yes, I do. And apparently, you're in the habit of bending them."

"If I was trying to bribe you, I'd use more than flowers and sweets." He lifted the lid on the pink box, revealing a variety of doughnuts—glazed, chocolate, twists and a pink cake one with colorful sprinkles.

"They look yummy," she said, "but I take my job seriously. I also took an oath to uphold the law."

Still, she peered into the box. She'd only had a light breakfast, and as she got a whiff of the sweet sugary smell, she was tempted.

She reached into her purse and pulled out one

of the dollar bills she kept tucked in a small pouch inside. "I'll tell you what. I'll buy that one with the pink frosting and candy sprinkles."

"Are you serious?" Steven laughed. "You think I'm a doughnut vendor now?"

"That's the only way I'll agree to take one."

For a moment, she thought he might lower the lid, but he took the dollar and waited for her to snatch the one she wanted.

She didn't wait to take a bite. "Hmm."

"You realize this never was meant to be a bribe."

"Then what is it?" she asked.

"A peace offering. I handled things badly on Saturday night, and I'm sorry."

She scanned the nearly empty lobby. "I'd rather not talk about that here."

"I realize that. Can we go for a walk?"

She lifted her arm to glance at her wristwatch, a college graduation gift from her parents. She had a meeting scheduled at ten, but she supposed it wouldn't hurt to take a few minutes to talk to him.

Steven nodded toward the glass door that led to the rose garden, a memorial for one of the beloved town founders, the first of many mayors who'd preceded her in office.

As they strolled toward a cement bench, Steven said, "I'm sorry for being a jerk the other night. You opened your heart to me, and I was so taken by surprise that I didn't offer you the support you deserved."

"I should have said something earlier, before…" She glanced at him, and when he nodded, she knew finishing her sentence wasn't necessary.

"Have you told anyone else yet?" he asked.

"I was going to talk to my parents, but I… haven't gotten around to it." Again, she glanced at Steven, and he nodded.

"Would you mind telling me more about the baby's father?" he asked.

"Why? I told you he's completely out of the picture."

"Yes, I know. But I'd like to be a better friend, a better listener."

So he wasn't going to run for the hills? They'd still be friends?

Ellie took a quick scan of the garden to assure herself no one was lurking nearby, that she was free to speak. "Mike and I had been dating for a while, and things got serious. But we'd been on different paths for months. He was doing a lot of traveling for work, and I was involved with local politics. We might have stuck it out, more as a habit. But…" She shook her head and continued. "One night, he told he me didn't want kids—ever. And that was a game changer for me. I mean, it's not like motherhood was at the top of my priority list, but eventually I would have wanted to have at least one child. So we broke up."

"When was that?"

"Four months ago. And I didn't even shed a tear. He flew to South America for an extended photo shoot, and I focused on Rambling Rose, as usual. But before long, I began counting the days and realized I'd gotten pregnant. He'd been downright adamant about not wanting a kid to screw up his life, so I knew he wouldn't be happy about it, but I figured I'd better tell him."

"What did he say?"

"He told me to get rid of it. I refused, and he said he was out, that I couldn't expect anything from him."

"Wow. What an ass."

"I realize that now. And I'm embarrassed by it. I mean, I should have picked up on his character flaws sooner than I did."

"Don't beat yourself up," Steven said. "We've all misjudged people. It happens."

"I know. I guess you could call it a lesson learned."

"Are you happy?" he asked. "I mean, about the baby?"

"Actually, I am. Some days I still can't believe it. By the middle of August, I'll be a mother."

"And a good one." Steven blessed her with a wink. "There's no doubt in my mind."

At times, she had a few doubts herself, even though her adoptive mom had set an amazing example, the best ever. Yet in spite of the outward sign of confidence Ellie had mastered years ago, she always felt as if she struggled between the past and the present.

It didn't happen very often these days, but occasionally a memory, a conversation, a voice would creep up on her and cause her to remember that her biological mom was a druggie who hadn't been married to her dad. And not just because he was serving a life sentence.

Thankfully, she'd been rescued from that dark world, but every now and then her adoptive father's question would come back to haunt her, to make her wonder if she'd ever be able to put it all behind her.

Honey, Ellie's a sweet kid. But do you think she inherited any bad genes from her biological parents?

From day one, Ellie had done her best to prove that she hadn't. Instead, she'd tried to be a reflection of the loving couple who'd adopted her—George Hernandez, a hardworking mechanic, and his wife, Alma, a devoted schoolteacher.

"Earth to Ellie."

She turned to Steven, who'd called her back to reality with a teasing grin.

"What's on your mind?" he asked. "I hope

you're not struggling about whether you should forgive me or not."

"I'm sorry. My mind drifted off, but don't worry. You're forgiven."

"Good." He studied her for a moment with eyes the color of the Texas sky. "Do you know whether it's a boy or a girl?"

Warmth filled her heart, and she placed her hand on her baby bump. "It's a boy."

"That's cool. Does he have a name?"

"Not yet. Daria, my friend, and I have been calling him Peanut ever since my first ultrasound, because that's what he looked like on the screen. But I'll probably name him George, after my dad."

"I'm sure that would make him proud."

"That's the plan." Her parents were pretty conservative. Still, she suspected their shock and disappointment wouldn't last very long. Daria was right. They'd be good grandparents.

"By the way," Steven said, "I gave away all but two of the tickets to the talent show at the high school on Thursday night. I thought you might want one."

"Actually, I would. Thanks."

"We could go together," he said.

Like a date? Probably not, but she'd better make it clear that she hadn't made that jump. "Can I meet you there?"

He seemed to ponder the question a little too long, then shrugged and said, "Sure. Why not?"

She glanced at her wristwatch, then at the glass door that led inside city hall. She needed to check in with Iris, the newly hired receptionist, and make sure that her ten o'clock meeting was still on.

"I'll let you go," Steven said. "Take the dough-nuts. They're not what you'd call a personal gift. They're for you to share with the office staff. You can do whatever you want with the roses, although I hope you'll keep them for yourself."

She glanced at the bouquet she still held, lifted them to her nose and took a sniff, relishing the strong fragrance. "They're beautiful. And they smell amazingly good."

They were also yellow, the color that signified friendship. A peace offering, he'd called them. She supposed she could live with that.

She and Steven were still friends. But for some reason, knowing that's all they'd ever be left her a little uneasy. And a wee bit sad.

At a quarter to seven on Thursday night, Steven waited for Ellie in front of the high school audi-torium. He'd been tempted to ask her to get a bite to eat with him before the talent show started, but that would have made the evening seem more like a date. And it wasn't.

It did kind of feel like one, though. As he stood

outside the open double doors, scanning the families and friends who were arriving to support the kids, his pulse kicked up a notch in anticipation. And the minute he spotted her approach, his heart damn near battered his chest.

As she hurried toward him, her cheeks flushed, he couldn't help but grin. She certainly had a thing about being on time, if not early. She also had a way of lighting up a room, no matter what she wore, be it a business suit or something more casual, like the black jeans and the long-sleeved pink blouse she had on tonight.

She might be pregnant, but he still found her attractive as hell. And while they weren't actually dating, that didn't mean they couldn't be friends. Right?

"I'm sorry I'm late," she said.

"You're ten minutes early," he argued, but he knew it was pointless.

"Daria's car wouldn't start. Her boss scheduled an unexpected meeting, so I had to drop her off first."

"No problem." Did that mean Ellie would have to cut their evening short to pick up her friend? "How's she going to get home?"

"She told me she'd catch a ride."

"Then let's go inside." Steven placed his hand on the small of Ellie's back to guide her toward the entrance. But touching her seemed a little too date-like, a little too intimate. So as she moved ahead of him, he let his fingers trail away.

Moments later, they were sitting in the two seats closest to the aisle, about six or seven rows from the stage.

Ellie leaned toward him, giving him an alluring whiff of her citrusy scent, and whispered, "I know this is a far cry from a Broadway show, but I had a good time last year. And I think you'll enjoy it."

She was right. Each performance was unique and entertaining.

A red-haired ventriloquist was a big hit, and so was a gymnast dressed in a clown costume who did flips and cartwheels across the stage. A couple of singers did a great job. Another tried hard but needed more practice. Several musicians played a variety of instruments, including the piano, a guitar, a trumpet and even a set of drums.

A barefoot girl wearing a white karate gi and a black belt showed off her martial arts skill. And a kid dressed in full cowboy garb, including chaps, carried a lariat onstage and performed rope tricks. But it was the last act that Steven liked best. A teenage boy and girl sang a duet from the Broadway musical *Annie Get Your Gun* that was worthy of a standing ovation. Their interaction on stage reminded him of the verbal banter he and Ellie often had. Not that either of them was all that competitive with the other, but he could imagine them singing "Anything you can do, I can do better."

As the oldest of the eight Fortune siblings, Steven was used to being the boss. And Ellie took her role as mayor seriously. She was tough and often underestimated, something he'd come to admire. It seemed only natural that two leaders like them often felt compelled to try and top each other.

The audience clapped and cheered at the end, then they all began to file out of the school auditorium. Steven figured he ought to offer to walk Ellie to her car, but he wasn't ready to say goodbye and send her off.

"I've got a real hankering for a hot fudge sundae," Steven said.

"A hankering, huh? I don't know, Mr. Fortune. You're starting to sound like a real Texan."

"Well, thank you, ma'am." He nodded toward the sidewalk that led to the shopping district. "The ice cream shop is just a couple of blocks down the street. Are you up for a short walk?"

Ellie brightened. "That actually sounds good to me. I have a real sweet tooth."

"You don't say." He laughed. "I guessed as much on Tuesday morning, when you zeroed in on that pink doughnut with candy sprinkles."

They moved through the throng of people and made their way across the street, which was unusually busy, thanks to the departing cars.

"By the way," Steven said, as they walked, "I've been thinking about all the people I met at Mariana's Market, and you're right. The longtime residents of Rambling Rose should be proud of the Fortune Brothers' development projects, and I want them to feel as if their voices have been heard." He glanced at Ellie, eager to see her reaction.

"Really?" Her eyes widened as if she could hardly believe the sudden turnaround. "You're going to alter your plans for the hotel?"

"Not exactly. I'm still one hundred percent behind the project. And I've heard nothing but positive reactions from the people who live in Rambling Rose Estates, but I really need to expand our support base. The way I see it, all I have to do is convince Mariana's crew that it's a good idea. Then it's only a matter of time before the planning commission gives us the green light."

Ellie grabbed him by the arm, pulled him to a halt, then circled in front of him and frowned. "Are you kidding me? You're more interested in persuading the people at Mariana's Market that you're right. I can't believe you're not going to consider their point of view at all."

Damn, she was pretty when she was worked up like that. But he wasn't going to bend to her—or to anyone—when it came to his personal project.

Steven sighed. "Have you even considered that I *could* be right?"

"No." She crossed her arms. "Not even *once*."

They stood like that for a moment, clearly at an impasse. Just like the song that had wrapped up the talent show. He almost made a joke of it. *Any stance you can take, I can take better.*

Something told him she wouldn't find it funny, though. And since they'd just become friends again, it wouldn't be wise to rock the boat.

He cast what he hoped was a disarming smile. "Like we've said before, Ellie. Maybe we should just agree to disagree."

Her expression softened, then she uncrossed her arms and returned to her place at his side. As he moved forward, she fell into step and they continued to walk along the sidewalk.

His arm brushed her shoulder a couple of times. If they'd been on an actual date, he would have reached for her hand.

Hell, he was tempted to do it anyway.

But he wouldn't.

"Will you meet me at Mariana's Market again this weekend?" he asked. "I'd like to set up a table where I can sit down with the locals and help them understand what the Fortune family has in mind for the project."

"I'll probably be there on Saturday. I like hanging out and talking to people. But I'm not going to sit at that table with you. I need to remain neutral, and I can't have even the appearance of favoritism where you and Fortune Brothers Construction are concerned. After all, optics are everything."

At that, he chuckled. "May I remind you that you're not the least bit neutral, and just about everyone in town knows how you really feel about the construction company and the hotel?"

"You do have a point there."

As they reached the Sweet Freeze, he opened the door for her, and she stepped inside. They weren't the only ones who'd had the idea of wrapping up their evening with an ice cream.

Moments later, Steven had ordered a triple fudge sundae, and Ellie chose a strawberry cone.

"And give her two scoops," he told the clerk.

They carried their desserts to a table at the rear of the shop and took a seat.

"Okay," Ellie said. "I'll stop by your display at Mariana's on Saturday."

He blinked in mock surprise. "All it took was a strawberry cone to convince you? I wish I would have known that sooner."

"I do love strawberries."

A grin tugged at his lips. "Does that mean you're going to be open-minded for a change?"

"What do you mean *for a change*? I'm always willing to look at both sides of a problem." She took a taste of her cone and then closed her eyes.

A rapturous expression crossed her face as she relished the taste, drawing his attention away from his own frozen chocolate concoction.

As he watched her lick that cone, his senses reeled, triggering thoughts of sex. If she continued to eat like that, as if she were making soft, breathless mewling sounds, he would end up watching her until his sundae melted into a soupy mess.

She drew the cone away from her mouth, then pointed the pink scoops at him. "Just for the record, you haven't swayed me in the least. But I'm curious about how you're going to reach out to the community—and how they'll take it. So count me in."

Oddly enough, he hadn't wanted to count her out. Even when they didn't see eye to eye, he was drawn to her. Under the circumstances, he ought to run like hell.

But he wasn't about to go anywhere, especially while she licked that blasted strawberry cone.

Ellie hadn't been to the Sweet Freeze in years, but she had a lot of nice memories here. Her mom used to teach school in Greenly, which was about twenty miles away, and she did a lot of tutoring after class and on Saturdays. So Ellie and her dad had spent a lot of time here—usually after a day at the playground, an afternoon matinee or following a softball game at the park.

She'd always had a fondness for ice cream, especially strawberry, but she couldn't remember it ever tasting this good. The sweet, cool treat really hit the spot. And it seemed to make her worries feel more like a couple of dust bunnies under the bed—still there but out of sight.

Steven leaned forward and lowered his voice. "I'd like to do something like this with you again."

Her lips parted, and she nearly dropped her cone onto the table. What was he suggesting?

"You want to meet at the Sweet Freeze?" she asked.

"Yes. I guess so. Or whatever."

She still wasn't sure what he meant. She had an idea, though. But she sure as heck wasn't going to make a guess, one that was more likely to be wrong.

So she skirted the question and delayed a response. "It's been a nice evening, hasn't it?"

Surely he didn't take the women he usually dated to high school talent shows and ice cream shops. She had to have connected the wrong dots. And, she admitted, that was actually a relief. A romantic liaison was out of the question, but the friend thing she could do.

"I had fun tonight," she added, against her better judgment.

He leaned back in his seat and smiled. "Surprisingly, I did, too."

The way he looked at her prickled her nerves and sent her blood racing. Was her deduction wrong? Was he actually talking about them going out, publicly? Okay, she was back to square one. And she wasn't sure what to say.

I'm pregnant. Remember?

And I'll soon look like I swallowed a basketball.

"So maybe we could go to a movie and have dinner?" he asked. "What do you think?"

"I think we should enjoy our ice cream." She scanned the immediate area, spotted a family placing their order up front, then lowered her voice. "It's one thing for us to be seen at community events, but I don't want people thinking we're… getting too chummy."

"Why should anyone care?"

She arched a brow. "Because I'm the mayor. And you and your family are at odds with the town."

"We're only at odds with some of the townspeople, although we're working on that."

"I hope so." She again scanned the ice cream shop, which was now close to empty. She doubted anyone could hear their conversation, but she didn't want to risk it and lowered her voice as a precaution. "There's one other reason. And when word…" She let her voice trail off, but he knew what she meant.

"You know," he said, his voice soft, low and

barely discernible, "the sooner you make the announcement, the better you'll feel."

He was right, she supposed. The pressure would be off, but she wasn't so sure she'd actually feel *better*. Not right away.

"So what did your parents say when you told them?" he asked. When she hesitated and looked down, he said, "You didn't tell them, did you?"

"Not yet."

"You do realize the cat will be out of the bag soon?"

"I know."

"Then you're better off telling them before they hear it from someone else."

Her eyes opened wide, and her heart raced. "Are *you* going to tell them?"

"No. Of course not. I gave you my word. What kind of guy do you think I am?"

In truth, she really had no idea. But she knew what kind of man he wasn't. One she should get involved with. Yet when he smiled at her like that, when he offered her friendship and support, not to mention his promise to keep her secret, her better judgment went up in smoke.

"On Saturday evening, after we spend the day at Mariana's Market, I'd like to take you out to dinner," he said. "Nothing fancy. Some place low-key and quiet. What do you think?"

That it was a crazy idea. Yet she was tempted beyond measure. She might be sorry for this later, but she gave a little shrug and said, "Sure. Why not?"

But after they left the Sweet Freeze and he walked her back to her car, after she turned on the ignition and headed home, she hoped she hadn't made another big mistake.

Chapter Seven

On Saturday morning, Steven and his brothers arrived at Mariana's Market early to set up a table before the shoppers arrived. Several tripods displayed photos of their completed projects and sketches of those still in the works. They also had a stack of colorful, glossy pamphlets ready to pass out to those who were interested or just plain curious.

An exhibit alone wasn't enough to draw much attention, so Steven decided to tempt passersby to stop at the table by offering complimentary refreshments—glasses of sweet tea and lemonade, along with platters of cookies he'd purchased from

Picard's Patisserie, the new French bakery that recently opened at the Shoppes.

After the successful grand opening nearly two weeks ago, one would think that shoppers would've flooded the specialty stores and eateries, something both Fortune Brothers Construction and the vendors had expected. Unfortunately, that hadn't been the case.

In an effort to boost sales and turn things around, Steven went out of his way to support and promote the various stores and businesses, which was why he'd placed a large order with Picard earlier that week.

"Fifteen dozen cookies ought to be enough," he'd told the short, balding baker. "I'd like a variety, but keep it simple. Nothing too fancy."

Steven hadn't wanted the people who frequented Mariana's Market to turn up their noses at something Picard had put his heart and soul into baking.

"I know just the thing," Picard said with a smile. "A lot of my specialties come from my *grandmaman's* recipes. She made cookies for me when I was a boy. You wait and see. Everyone will love them."

Last night, after Steven had picked up the carefully packed boxes from the bakery and climbed behind the wheel of his SUV, he'd tried one. Picard had been right; they were delicious. But they might be more elegant and worldly than Mariana's patrons were used to.

Now, as it neared ten o'clock on Saturday morning, people had begun to stop by the Fortunes' table to check out the multicolored macarons, French butter cookies and lemon madeleines, a costly purchase, even with the loyalty discount Picard had given them.

An older man wearing worn denim overalls and a red baseball cap—a farmer, Steven suspected—squinted as he peered at the table. "What the hell are those?"

"Cookies," Callum said. "Give 'em a try."

"How much?" the guy asked.

Steven lifted one of the trays so the man could get a better look at the variety of cookies. "No charge. They're complimentary. Go ahead and have one. Or take a few."

The farmer grunted, picked up a pink macaron, studied it for a moment and popped it into his mouth.

Steven reached for one of the pamphlets to give him, but the man slowly shook his head, lifted a weathered hand and waved him off. "Don't need it, Mr. Fortune. I'll take a free cookie, but I ain't buyin' what you're trying to sell." Then he turned and walked away.

Steven was still holding the unwanted pamphlet when Ellie approached the table. She'd dressed casually today in a pink-and-white-striped blouse, black denim jeans and a pair of sneakers. She also wore a pretty pout, which, for once, wasn't directed at Steven. Instead, she seemed a bit annoyed with the gangly black puppy she'd brought with her.

Ellie gave a gentle tug on the red leash to encourage the little rascal to come her way, but the distracted pup was more interested in its surroundings and the people milling through the marketplace.

Steven set down the pamphlet, left Callum at the table and strode toward Ellie, glad to see her.

"This must be Tank," he said.

She blew out a sigh and tucked a long, glossy strand of dark hair behind her ear. "I'm puppy-sitting. Daria's boss asked her to attend a business meeting with him in Houston, and Tank gets into too much trouble when he's left home alone. So I thought I'd better bring him with me."

"Didn't she have a business meeting with her boss last night?" Steven had never met Daria and didn't know anything about the relationship she had with her employer. Not that it was any of his business. Didn't Ellie find it odd that they would meet out of town—and on a weekend?

"Actually," Ellie said, "her boss called all of his employees together to announce that he's selling the car wash. Daria is the bookkeeper, so he asked her to go to Houston with him to meet the buyers. He thought she'd be able to answer any financial questions they might have."

"That makes sense. Hopefully, the new owners will let her keep her job."

"Daria doesn't think they will. They have several other car washes, so they probably already have a bookkeeper or accountant in place."

"That's too bad. Tell her that once the hotel nears completion, there will be a lot of job opportunities. In fact, that's what we've been telling people who stop by our table."

Ellie cut a glance at their display, where Callum was talking to two women in their mid-forties. The ladies appeared to be more interested in choosing a couple of cookies from the platters than they were in listening to anything Callum had to say about the hotel.

They were going to need community support if they wanted to get approval from the planning commission, which was the reason they'd set up the table in the middle of the marketplace in the first place. But it wasn't a good idea to open with the hotel. If Steven had been the one talking to them, he first would've tried to interest them in Paz, the spa that would be opening in a few weeks. Then he'd point out the restaurant they were building for his sisters, which would open in May. After he'd gotten their attention, he would have introduced the prospective hotel.

Sharing that strategy with his brother could wait. Now that Ellie was here, Steven was eager to steer away from the company/business chatter.

"How's your effort to kumbaya with the locals going?" she asked. "Have you made any new friends yet?"

Not really, but he didn't tell her that. He didn't want to hear her say *I told you so*. "It's early yet. The day's just getting started."

Ellie twisted the loop end of the leash, bit down on her bottom lip then asked, "Can I talk to you for a minute?"

"Sure."

"Privately?" She nodded to the right, away from any people walking by.

Steven took the first step, but Ellie's tug of the leash didn't faze Tank, so she stooped, picked up the noncompliant puppy and walked a few feet until they were out of earshot.

"What's going on?" Steven asked.

"Something's come up, and I can't go out to dinner with you tonight."

He might have let it go at that and asked if they could try again later in the week, but her eye twitched and tension stretched across her brow. He zeroed in on her big brown eyes and tried to read the subtext behind her words, but he wasn't having any luck. "What aren't you telling me?"

"Nothing. Not really. I…" She tore her gaze away from his and bent to place Tank back on the ground. After giving the pup a scratch behind the ear, she returned to an upright position and shrugged. "I already told you. I'm puppy-sitting, remember?"

Yes, but there had to be more to it than that. He suspected that she was having second thoughts about having dinner with him, about being seen with him in a social setting. He couldn't be sure, though. "There's a place on the corner of Main and Jefferson that serves burgers and salads. They have a few tables set up curbside and a sign out front that says they're pet friendly. So Tank can come along, too. That is, if he's the only reason you're dragging your feet."

She didn't answer right away, and while he waited, studying the silky strands of her hair, the thick dark lashes that framed her big brown eyes, the tilt of her chin, sexual awareness slammed into him and sent his blood pounding.

Did she feel it, too? Were the same arousing thoughts zapping through her brain?

She sucked in a deep breath and blew it out. "Okay, Steven. Here's the deal. Going out to dinner with you would be cool. And fun. But it would feel like a date, and there are a hundred reasons why that isn't a good idea."

He'd already considered each one. Yet none of them seemed to matter right now, even if they should.

"What's holding you back?" he asked.

She placed her free hand on her stomach, caressed the slight bulge for a moment, then let her fingers trail away.

The baby. Okay. She had a point. And it should give him pause, but it didn't. For some reason, he liked her. And he wanted to spend more time with her.

Before he could respond, a loud, angry voice sounded behind them, coming from the Fortune Brothers' table.

A big man in his late thirties shook his finger at Callum. "You good-for-nothing piece of crap. You Fortunes think you can pass out treats and sweet-talk the good folks of Rambling Rose into believing that you're on our side. But that's a crock. You only have your own interests and profits at heart."

Steven and his brothers could hold their own in a fight, even with a hulk who looked as if he'd once been a linebacker for the Dallas Cowboys. But he'd better stand beside Callum anyway, ready to offer backup, whether it was calm words or a physical stance.

Ellie stopped him before he could take a step and handed him the end of the leash. "Take this." Then she marched toward the hothead.

She reached him just as he pointed to the platters and said, "You can take those cookies and shove them up—"

"Jackson!" Ellie called out in a voice nearly as strong and loud as the one she'd just quieted.

The bulky, broad-shouldered giant turned to the mayor and folded his arms across his chest, resting them on what appeared to be the start of a beer belly.

"You're making a scene," she said.

"Maybe I am, but somebody's got to stand up to the Fortunes and tell them how it is. You've seen how they've moved into town and started buying up property and turning things upside down. Hell, they're acting as if they own the whole damn place."

"They've done some good things, too," Ellie said.

Jackson chuffed. "I can see they've already got to you and worn you down."

"Slow down," Ellie said. "Just the other day, I talked to your sister. Her son, *your nephew*, was treated for the intestinal flu and severe dehydration at the Rambling Rose Pediatric Center."

Jackson let out a half-assed snort. "The doctors

and nurses helped Joey. Not the Fortunes. They just prettied up the building."

"Come with me," Ellie told the red-faced man. "I want to talk to you. Away from the crowd."

Jackson held his ground for a moment. Then he turned and reluctantly followed the much smaller mayor out of the hearing range of anyone near the table. But still close enough for Steven to be privy to their conversation.

"No one loves this town more than I do," she told Jackson. "But as your mayor, I need to look out for *all* the townspeople. And that means those who live in Rambling Rose Estates, as well as the store owners at the Shoppes and Fortune Brothers Construction."

"Yeah, Ellie. I know. But you can't let 'em ruin our town."

"The Fortunes have done more than just 'pretty up' Rambling Rose. They've put our friends and neighbors to work, either directly or indirectly."

The man's brow furrowed, and he glanced down at his feet.

"Jackson, you trusted me with your vote. Now you need to trust me to lead Rambling Rose, to make compromises when necessary and to stand firm when bottom lines matter."

When Ellie looked up and realized Steven had been listening, she took Jackson aside, placed her hand on his shoulder and spoke privately with him.

The chat didn't last long. Maybe only a minute or two. Then Jackson nodded and walked away, his big, broad shoulders slumped.

Ellie remained where she stood and watched his retreat. Then she returned to Steven's side and reached for Tank's leash.

He handed it to her. "That was unbelievable."

Her brow twitched. "What was? Jackson's tirade? He's not the only one in town with strong feelings about your projects and the changes that are being made in the community."

"Actually," Steven said, "I was talking about *you*. I'm amazed at the way you handled that guy. Your persuasive techniques are your superpower. I saw you do it at the grand opening of the Shoppes, when you stopped the protest. And now this. So thank you. Again."

"You're welcome. But that wasn't anything special. It was just me. And what I do."

No, it was more than that. A lot more. And he suspected she knew it, too. "You went to bat for us, and I want to thank you by taking you to dinner."

"You don't owe me anything. Jackson has a loud mouth, and he gets worked up easily when he thinks there's been an injustice done. He doesn't always think before getting angry, but he has a big heart, especially when it comes to his family. So I took him aside and asked what his mother would think about him raising a ruckus in public. As I suspected, he backed right down."

"You really know your neighbors."

"Yes, I do. Anyway, it wasn't a big deal."

"I think it was," Steven said. "I don't like public altercations. You and I may not agree on many things, but we both want peace in our community. And a blowup at Mariana's Market, especially today, would make the company look bad. Believe it or not, the Fortunes are well thought of in Fort Lauderdale. I might not be a Fortune by blood, but I'm proud to bear the name. And I don't want my family and the construction company to be frowned upon in Rambling Rose."

She arched a single brow, clearly skeptical of his claim.

"All right," he said. "I'll admit that some of the townspeople don't like us—or trust us. But we're working on that."

She offered him a smile, then glanced down at the ground, where Tank was resting his head on his paw. Surprisingly, he looked to be taking a nap.

"So how about dinner tonight?" Steven asked again. "I'll pick you up. Or you can meet me there."

"I don't know…" she said.

"Over the last few weeks, we've become friends. Most of the community is beginning to see that, too. So don't worry about being seen with me in a social setting. Friends do things together all the time, and that includes sharing a meal."

She glanced down at the puppy sleeping at her feet, then looked up and grinned. "I'll ask one of the neighbor kids to look after Tank. So it doesn't matter where we eat. I'm up for burgers, Italian or whatever."

"Since you're giving me a choice, then let's go to Osteria Oliva."

Ellie furrowed her brow. "I've never heard of that. Where is it?"

"It's the new Italian restaurant that opened at the Shoppes. And before you object and say it's too trendy or ritzy, I have a good reason for wanting to eat there. Carla Vicente, the new owner, lost her father a few months ago. The restaurant had been his dream, and now she's determined to make a go of it as a tribute to him. But it's been a struggle."

"Why?"

"Carla doesn't have many customers yet. Hopefully, once the foot traffic at the Shoppes picks up and word spreads, she'll do all right."

"So you're trying to help."

Steven shrugged. "I guess you could say that helping is *my* superpower."

"Apparently, there's a lot I don't know about you." She studied him for a moment, her eyes twinkling with an unspoken thought. He'd give anything to know what she was thinking. Or feeling.

"Just for the record," she added, "you can be pretty persuasive, too."

"I have four younger sisters, so that's a skill I had to hone early. But I have to admit, you're not easy to sway."

"I know." She offered him a smile. "But in this case, you did. I'd like to support Carla, too. So tell me what time, and I'll meet you there."

"How about six? I'm sure she'll be thrilled to have the Rambling Rose mayor eat at her restaurant."

"Sounds good." Ellie stooped to pick up the sleepy puppy. "I'll see you tonight."

As she turned to walk away, her arms full with a squirming puppy, Steven couldn't help but shake his head and grin. He and Ellie might be at odds most of the time, but she actually had become his friend, and he was really looking forward to spending the evening with her.

And if he played his cards right, maybe they'd become more than friends.

After parking at the Shoppes, Ellie made her way into the lobby, a smile on her lips and a zing in her steps. She continued past the specialty shops on the first floor to the far end, where Osteria Oliva was located. She hated to admit it, but she was looking forward to having dinner with Steven.

He'd been right. The two of them had, surprisingly, become friends. And good ones, it seemed.

As she neared the restaurant, footsteps sounded behind her. She glanced over her shoulder to see Steven approach, a dazzling grin on his face. She stopped to wait for him to catch up.

From the black Stetson on his head to the boots on his feet, her newfound friend was looking more like a cowboy every day. And more handsome than he had a right to be.

He placed a hand on her shoulder, and the warmth of his gentle touch sent a coil of heat spiraling to her core, stirring up feelings that were a far cry from platonic.

"Thanks for waiting up," he said, as they continued on together. "I think you'll like this place, especially since it's special and trendy, but not fancy."

As they stepped through the arched entry, Ellie scanned the sunflower-yellow walls adorned with colorful European-style artwork, each with a dark frame that matched the wooden tables and chairs. A hand painted mural on the side wall depicted a vineyard and a quaint cottage. To the right of the cash registers, a small grocery section displayed imported products, such as olive oils, dry pasta, sauces, herbs and Italian wines.

There was a lot to like about Osteria Oliva, but Steven hadn't stretched the truth when he'd mentioned the lack of patrons. For a Saturday night, the new eatery was practically dead.

A matronly woman, her silver-threaded dark hair pulled into a neat and tidy bun, greeted them at the door. "It's nice to see you again, Steven."

"This time I brought a friend." He turned to Ellie, his hand still lingering on her back, his touch sending tingles down her spine. "This is Ellie Hernandez, the mayor of Rambling Rose."

Carla extended her arm and gave Ellie's hand a warm, two-handed shake. "It's nice to meet you. Thank you for coming."

"Steven raves about the food, so I'm glad to be here."

Carla swept her arm out toward the nearly empty room, where one older couple sat near the mural. "Please, sit anywhere you like."

Steven ushered Ellie to the back of the room, where they took their seats at a table for two.

A waiter dressed in black slacks and a crisply pressed white button-down shirt stood off to the side. He gave them a moment to settle in before approaching their table with two menus.

"Can I get you something to drink?" he asked.

"I'll have a glass of your Chianti Classico Reserva," Steven said.

Ellie smiled at the waiter. "Just water for me."

He nodded. When he left them to look over the menus, Ellie checked out the offerings—salads, sandwiches and European-style pizza. She suspected the locals who'd lived in town all their lives would find the food appealing. The prices weren't especially steep, either. But those people weren't shopping at the high-end stores, which meant they weren't going to stumble upon Osteria Oliva.

Moments later, when the waiter returned with a basket of fresh focaccia sprinkled with rosemary, they placed their orders—a sausage calzone for Steven and the vegetarian antipasto salad for Ellie.

"So what's new at Fortune Brothers Construction?" Ellie asked. "Any recent land grabs? Any new renovation projects in the works?"

"Not at the moment." He picked up the bread basket, offered it to her and waited until she chose a piece. "We're going to have to plan a retirement party, though. I knew it was coming. Our office manager made the official announcement this morning. I'm happy for him, but he's been an incredible asset, especially during our move to Texas. It'll be hard to replace him."

Ellie opened her mouth to recommend Daria for the position, but she didn't like the idea of her best friend going to work for the enemy—even though Steven no longer felt like one. Then again, Daria had student loans to pay back and would be out of a job once the car wash sold.

"Let me know when you start looking to replace the office manager. Or if you have to shuffle people around and another position opens up. My friend Daria doesn't have a ton of experience, but she has a college degree. She's also a hard worker and loyal. I'm sure she'd like to apply."

"Tell her to give me a call next week," Steven said.

Once their dinner was served, they continued to talk. And this time, for a change, without their usual bickering.

Steven told her about growing up in Fort Lauderdale, especially when he was a teenager. He might have done well academically, played sports and had a weekend construction job, but he'd still managed to have fun—and to get into mischief.

"How'd you manage to stay out of trouble?" she asked.

"It wasn't so hard in high school, but I got in plenty of trouble when I was in eighth grade." He tossed her a playful grin. "One day, we had a substitute teacher in math, and the guy didn't appreciate my sense of humor. So he sent me to the principal's office. More often than not, during P.E., the coach used to make me run extra laps for being a wise-ass. But the last time I got into trouble, my dad grounded me, and that was a real game changer for me."

"What did you do?"

"One of my buddies invited me to his family's country club to play golf. I was driving the cart a little too fast and ran it into a tree. My dad wasn't happy about it. He paid for the repair bill, but I had to pay him back—with interest." Steven rested his elbows on the table and leaned toward her, his blue eyes glimmering with mirth. "Now it's your turn. I admitted to a lot of stuff, and you just sat there smiling, taking it all in as if you'd never met such an entertaining hellion. Didn't you ever get into trouble?"

Ellie glanced around the empty restaurant, pretending to watch for eavesdroppers, then leaned forward and lowered her voice. "Don't tell anyone, but I got a B-plus one semester in chemistry, which screwed up my chance to be the valedictorian."

Steven feigned surprise, placed a hand on his chest and gasped. "Seriously? That bad, huh?"

They both laughed, but it was true. That's about the worst thing she'd done while in school. And if truth be told, she'd cried when she'd realized that B-plus had lowered her GPA enough to allow Jose Rivera to snag the coveted award.

Funny how it seemed a little insignificant now. And she found it even funnier that she'd really enjoyed her evening with Steven tonight.

After he paid the bill and left a tip, they headed toward the lobby doors that would take them to the parking lot.

"Thank you for dinner," Ellie said. "Now I owe you one."

"Sounds good to me. Just tell me where and when. Or, better yet, give me your address, and I'll pick you up at your house."

She didn't want anyone to think they were dating, and while they really weren't, they sure seemed to be tiptoeing around it. So she came up with a better option—if he was interested. "There's an event in San Antonio I need to attend on Tuesday afternoon. If you can get the time off and don't mind hanging out with me for a boring hour or two, we could have an early dinner in the city."

"Sure. I don't have a lot going on Tuesday. What time do you want to leave?"

"One o'clock. It shouldn't last too long—an hour or two at the most. And if we don't dawdle over dinner, we should be back in Rambling Rose before it gets too late."

"Sounds good." Steven scanned the nearly empty parking lot. "Where's your car?"

"It's just to the right, next to the gray Lexus."

"I'll walk with you," he said.

When they reached her trusty Honda, she thanked him again for dinner and a nice evening.

"I'm glad you enjoyed it. I hope you'll help Carla out by spreading the word about her restaurant at Mariana's Market."

"Will do."

Ellie was about to turn away to reach for the door handle when Steven cupped her cheek. His gaze locked on hers like a laser, startling her. Tempting her.

He leaned forward, and while she ought to stop him, she couldn't seem to move. Her lips parted, and her heart raced. He kissed her lightly, sweetly—almost like a friend—at first. But as his tongue slipped into her mouth, seeking and finding her own, her hormones spun out of control.

Thankfully, after a surreal moment of sexual bliss, her brain kicked into gear. She placed her hand against his broad chest, felt the strong, steady beat of his heart, and pushed back, breaking the kiss almost as quickly as it started.

"We can't," she said. "I can't…"

"Why? Are you worried that someone will see us?"

"There's that. Yes."

And so much more.

It was too much. Too fast. Too soon.

"Ellie," he said, "you didn't do anything wrong. If you're worried about appearances, you shouldn't be. Even public figures are allowed to have a private life."

"It's not that simple." She stepped back and lowered her voice. "It's one thing to be an unwed mother, but I don't want to be one that's dating." Talk about flitting from one man's bed to another. Not that she'd planned to jump into bed with Steven, but she'd certainly kissed him. And she'd liked it. A lot.

"This is the twenty-first century, Ellie. People have children out of wedlock all the time. It's not a big deal."

"I know. But to me, it is."

"What makes you different?" he asked.

"It's hard to explain. I guess you could say that, try as I might, I still carry a little baggage from my early childhood years."

"Like what?" he asked.

The question sparked memories she'd like to forget. The shabby apartment where she once lived. The stained, threadbare green carpet. The knocks at the front door. The men who stopped by daily to visit her mother, a woman she'd dubbed Liz once she'd gotten a real mom.

Child Protective Services had taken her out of that apartment and that life when she was six, but she still recalled the neighbors' disapproving whispers and felt her mother's shame as if it had been her own.

That's why it mattered what people thought of her and how they'd react to her news. What would they say if she were to date a man who wasn't her baby's father, a man who bore the Fortune name?

"I'm sorry," she said. "I really like you, Steven, but under the circumstances, I think we should remain friends. At least for the time being."

He studied her for a moment, as if he hadn't heard her, then he tossed her a carefree grin. "Okay. Friends it is. I'll meet you at city hall a little before one on Tuesday."

Stunned that he still intended to go with her to San Antonio, she merely nodded as she climbed into her car and closed the door.

Steven Fortune was the last man in the world she ought to be attracted to, especially now.

Just friends, he'd said. And that sounded good. But how was that ever going to work when she couldn't deny his strong sexual appeal?

Chapter Eight

I really like you, but...

Some might consider a comment like that to be a brush-off, a way for a woman to let them down easy, but Steven knew Ellie had feelings for him. He'd seen it in her eyes, heard it in her laugh and felt it in her touch.

He liked her, too—as a verbal sparring partner and as a friend. And he certainly found her attractive. It was too early to tell if anything romantic would develop, but he felt drawn to her, and the chemistry was definitely there. Oddly enough, her reluctance to date or to be seen with him in public made him all the more determined to see her privately.

The way he saw it, the only thing standing in their way was political in nature. That's why it had both surprised and pleased him when she'd asked him to go with her to that event in San Antonio.

Now that Tuesday had rolled around, he took a cue from her and arrived at city hall at a quarter to one, which was on time by her standards. Rather than enter the building and ask for her, which seemed like the proper thing to do, he opted to respect her privacy and call her cell.

When she answered, he said, "I'm in the parking lot."

"I'll be right there."

And she was. He'd hardly shut off his ignition when he spotted her coming out the door and striding toward his SUV.

She was dressed in her typical business attire— a black suit and heels. She hadn't buttoned the blazer, nor had she tucked in the white blouse. Probably to hide her baby bump, which seemed a bit pronounced today. A good sign that her son was growing, that she had a healthy pregnancy.

As she climbed into the passenger seat, the hem of her skirt lifted and provided him with a glimpse of her shapely legs. The alluring sight didn't surprise him. His visceral reaction did.

"You look nice." He tossed her a smile. "As usual."

"Thanks." She adjusted her seat belt and tugged at her blouse.

As he pulled out of the parking lot and headed out of town, he said, "So tell me. What kind of event is this?"

"It's a gathering of mayors and other city officials from several nearby counties. The idea is for us to join forces in a cooperative effort to increase tourism in this part of the state."

"That's interesting. And a little ironic, don't you think?" A smile tugged at his lips, and he stole a glance across the seat. When he caught her eye, he winked. "Do you plan to join that effort or oppose it?"

"Very funny. But I suppose that's a fair question, since I haven't given you any reason to think I'm pro-tourism. Actually, I am. I just don't want to draw in the wrong kind of tourist to our town. I'd like to hear what they have to say, but don't worry. After the initial speeches, I'm going to leave. That way, we can have an early dinner."

Just as Ellie predicted, the few speeches didn't last much longer than an hour or so, although Steven suspected that he'd found them to be more interesting than Ellie had.

At the end of the presentation, the San Antonio mayor thanked them all for coming. "If you'll step through the open door into the adjoining room, you'll find several displays of various businesses within our counties and interesting places that visitors might like to see while in the area."

Steven leaned toward Ellie and whispered, "I know you said you'd be ready to cut out early, but would you mind if I took a look in that room?"

"Not at all. I'd like to see the displays, too."

As they entered what appeared to be a small exhibition hall, one business caught Steven's immediate attention. The Mendoza Winery out of Austin had set up four wine-tasting booths in each corner of the room. "Well, I'll be darned. I didn't expect to see any of my relatives here. Come on, I'd like to introduce you to my cousin Schuyler and her husband, Carlo Mendoza, the vice president of the Mendoza Winery. I met them last year, when we attended a wedding."

"Who got married?" Ellie asked, as she followed Steven to one of several wine bars.

"Jerome Fortune, once known as Gerald Robinson. He finally married the love of his life, a woman he'd dated forty years earlier. It's a little complicated. I'll explain more later."

When Steven and Ellie approached the booth where Carlo and Schuyler had displayed several bottles of red wine, Steven called out, "Fancy meeting you two here."

Carlo looked up, and when he spotted Steven, he flashed his trademark grin and extended his hand. "Our new motto is 'Have winery, will travel.'"

Schuyler, who looked especially pretty today in a classic red dress, smiled brightly. "Hey, Steven. It's good to see you. I didn't realize you were involved in politics."

"Only by association," he said. "Let me introduce you to my friend Ellie Hernandez, the mayor of Rambling Rose."

After the three took turns shaking hands, Steven turned to Ellie and said, "Before Schuyler married Carlo, she was a Fortune, although her family went by the name of Fortunado."

"We're offering each city official a case of Mendoza wine," Carlo said. "So Ellie, if you'll let me know when you're leaving, I'll have it carried out to your car."

"Thank you," Ellie said. "That's very generous."

Carlo placed his hand on his wife's back. "I wish I could take credit for the brilliant promotional idea, but Schuyler is always coming up with new ways for us to spread the word about our wines."

"When Carlo and I met last June," Steven told Ellie, "we found out we had a lot in common. We both hail from Florida."

"They also love wine," Schuyler added. "And they're huge Miami Dolphins fans."

Ellie let out a little gasp, feigning surprise at the audacity. "Keep your voices down. Everyone here is either a staunch fan of the Dallas Cowboys or the Houston Texans. I'd hate to see y'all get thrown out of here."

"Speaking of getting thrown out," Carlo said to Steven, "or rather cuffed and dragged out of town, what'd you think of Charlotte Robinson's final act at Jerome and Deborah's wedding?"

"What a wedding crasher." Steven let out a little whistle, then offered an explanation to Ellie. "Charlotte is Jerome's ex-wife. She was an angry, deceitful woman before they divorced, but she became completely unhinged afterward and took out her vengeance on a lot of people in the Fortune family."

"That's right," Carlo said. "In fact, now that I think about it, Ellie, you probably either know or have heard of Paxton Price. He used to be the sheriff, but he was recently elected mayor of Paseo."

"We've met a couple of times. He's a nice guy. I believe he was once a Dallas detective."

"That's right," Schuyler said. "During the ceremony, Charlotte came in screaming and waving a gun. After firing it in the air, she took Pax's future wife, Georgia Fortune, hostage."

"Oh no." Ellie's eyes grew wide. "That's horrible."

"It *truly* was," Schuyler said. "But luckily, Georgia was rescued unharmed, and Jerome and Deborah were able to get married the next day."

"I hope Charlotte is still in that psychiatric hospital," Steven said.

"I'm sure she is." Carlo reached for an uncorked bottle of merlot and poured a couple of ounces into each of two wineglasses. "After the fire, vandalism, cut brake lines and then a kidnapping, she'll probably remain there or in prison for a very long time."

Schuyler took the wine and handed it to Ellie. Steven expected her to decline, but she took it. Probably to be polite—or to put up a facade. He didn't think she'd drink it.

"That wedding was very nice," Schuyler said, "but it was the craziest one I've ever attended. And the biggest. Each and every known Fortune was invited to a two-week-long celebration leading up to the ceremony in Paseo."

"Seriously?" Ellie took a sip of wine, although she barely made a dent in the small pour. "Where'd they all stay? I mean, Paseo isn't a large town."

"Believe it or not," Steven said, "we camped out in a field on Deborah's ranch. You should have seen all the travel trailers, tents and luxury motor homes."

Schuyler handed Steven a glass of merlot. "Wasn't it cool to meet all the Fortune relatives?"

He wouldn't call it cool. There'd been a lot of them, and it had taken a while to learn their names and connections, especially since he and his family had always kept to themselves.

"It was definitely interesting," he said.

"Have you heard anything from Gary Fortune's side of the family?" Schuyler asked.

"I've been approached by Adam and Kane, two of his sons. They're hoping to get involved in some of the projects my brothers and I are spearheading in Rambling Rose."

Moments later, Paxton Price approached the wine bar. The tall, broad-shouldered man with a stocky build first greeted the Mendozas, then Steven. When he spotted Ellie, he grinned. "How're things going in Rambling Rose?"

"Other than being a little overrun by the rich and the famous?" She gave Steven a playful nudge. "We're hanging in there."

Pax chuckled. "I hear you. Same thing happened in Paseo, but it's not so bad, especially when you fall in love with one of them."

Ellie, who'd never seemed to be at a loss for words, flushed, her cheeks a pretty shade of pink.

"If I'd known this was going to turn out to be a family reunion," Pax said with a grin, "I would have asked Georgia to come with me."

Before anyone could respond, a couple others moseyed up to the wine bar, and Schuyler gave them her full attention.

Steven placed his empty glass on a tray set off

to the side and then addressed Carlo. "Ellie and I had better move on and let you two get back to work. But you can expect a call from me next week. I'd like to order a case of that merlot. It was amazingly good."

"You got it," Carlo said.

As Steven and Ellie turned to walk away, Schuyler called him back. "Steven, why don't you plan a visit to Austin one of these days?"

"I just might do that. I'd love to tour the winery."

"And bring Ellie," his cousin added. "I'll take her around the city and show her all the hot spots."

"Sounds like fun. I'll talk to you later." Steven stole a glance at Ellie. He wondered how she felt about being included in the invitation. He couldn't tell by looking, but there'd be time for them to talk about it over dinner—or on the way home.

As he scanned the city officials studying the displays that had been set around the room, he realized Schuyler wasn't the only one who'd assumed Steven and Ellie were a couple.

Unlike Schuyler, who seemed so accepting, the two women standing near a display of the San Antonio River Walk were eyeing them a little too carefully, a hint of disapproval in their expressions.

As Ellie and Steven walked around the room, she clutched the stem of her wineglass, pretending that she was actually drinking when she'd only taken a single sip. The merlot was good, though. Very good.

It might be fun to go with Steven to Austin and tour the Mendoza Winery. But being the mayor kept her busy. Her calendar was pretty full. And once the baby came…well, she wouldn't have much free time at all.

She took another scan of the displays that had been set up around the room and headed toward one that highlighted San Antonio's famous River Walk. She wanted to check out the nearby restaurants. It would be nice to eat near the water.

As she crossed the room, she spotted two well-groomed women looking at her and whispering. She recognized the snooty brunette wearing black slacks and a red blazer, although she couldn't remember her name. They'd probably run across each other a couple of times but had never been formally introduced.

"Like I told you before," the middle-aged brunette said to the blonde standing beside her, "she might be young and pretty, but no one takes her seriously."

Blondie let out a little snort, then lowered her voice, but she didn't speak quietly enough. "The men do, but for all the wrong reasons. All they can talk about is how beautiful she is, how sexy they find her. And they seem to agree that it'd be worth a move to Rambling Rose, just to see her more often."

Ellie's hearing had always been good, which had come in handy more times than not. Steven wasn't too far from the women. Had he picked up their conversation?

"She's not that sexy anymore," the brunette added. "Check out her waistline. She's getting thick in the belly."

"You're right. She didn't tuck in her blouse. Probably because she can't button her pants these days." Blondie covered her mouth to stifle a laugh. "Too much fast food. Or too many trips to the bakery."

Ellie's cheeks warmed, and her stomach clenched. Normally she had pretty thick skin, but pregnancy hormones must have gotten the better of her, pushing her to react. Instead of letting the rude comments pass, she approached the two catty women.

"Body shaming is frowned on these days," she said. "It actually makes those doing the shaming look bad. And that's not wise, especially if either of you has political aspirations. I suggest you take a class on how to be more PC. And while you're at it, you should learn how to conduct yourselves at public events. A little tact and kindness goes a long way."

"I'm sorry," Blondie said. "We didn't mean for you to hear that. We thought we'd kept our voices down."

"You didn't. But that's not the point. You shouldn't judge a person's character on their outward appearance. You're more apt to be wrong than right."

Ellie was about to turn away when Steven placed his hand on her shoulder, bolstering her with his presence, providing his support.

"Ellie Hernandez is the most beautiful woman in this room," Steven said, "inside and out. Unlike you two, she doesn't have a mean or jealous bone in her body."

Blondie seemed noticeably chastised—and perhaps a bit sorry.

On the other hand, the brunette lifted her finger and pointed at Ellie as if she were a parent scolding a child. "You're not going to be able to hide it forever, Ms. Hernandez. I can see the signs. How long before Rambling Rose realizes that the mayor has a bun in the oven?"

Shock and mortification struck Ellie like a wallop to the diaphragm, sucking the air out of her lungs. It took her a moment to recover, then she gathered up her battered pride and stood tall. "My private life is none of your business. Nor is it your concern."

Then she turned and walked away, leaving Steven with the two horrid women. She had no idea what he'd do or what he'd say—if anything—but she wasn't going to stick around to find out.

A couple of beats later, he was by her side.

"Are you okay?" he asked.

"Yes, I'm fine. But I need to get out of here. *Now.*"

Ellie hadn't mentioned a word about going out to an early dinner. She'd just insisted that they leave. But Steven couldn't blame her for that. The gossipy women had turned his stomach, and even though he'd had a light lunch, he wasn't hungry, either.

As he pulled his SUV out of the parking lot and began the drive back to Rambling Rose, he glanced across the seat at Ellie. "You doing okay?"

"Yes."

He didn't believe her, but he held his tongue and let silence fill the cab. He didn't blame Ellie for retreating from San Antonio. Her secret was out—or at least, someone had noticed her pregnancy.

Each time he stole a glance her way and saw her troubled expression, he wanted to reach out and take her hand, tell her it was going to be okay. But she leaned her head against the passenger window, pulling away from him. He figured he'd better give her some space.

By the time they reached the city hall parking lot, where she'd left her car, he couldn't hold his tongue any longer. "There's something I want to tell you."

She turned to him, but she didn't speak. Instead, she questioned him with her eyes.

"Those women were rude, and their comments hurt you and were totally uncalled-for. But you held your head high, and that's not always easy to do when people are mean and poke their noses where they don't belong. I'm proud of you, Ellie."

"Thanks." She gave a slight shoulder shrug. "I can handle the cattiness, the smirks and the laughter when it's directed at me personally. But I don't want my past or my private life to distract people from what's important."

"What's *really* important," he said, "is that you take care of yourself. You have a baby on the way, and you need to focus on that."

She looked up at him like a startled doe in a thicket. Her lips and chin trembled. Tears welled in her eyes, and for once, her gaze held no resistance, no argument, no objection. Rather, her vulnerability peered out at him, turning him to mush and leaving him vulnerable, too.

In an effort to show his support, he leaned across the seat and cupped her jaw. Then he drew her face toward him and placed a kiss on her brow. He wasn't sure how he expected her to react. A smile, maybe. But she burst into tears, shocking the hell out of him.

You'd think that he'd have mastered how to deal with a crying female, especially after he helped to raise four little sisters, but this situation was different. Ellie was different.

"Aw, honey. Don't…" Words failed him. The tough, sharp politician he could handle. This soft, sweet, hurting woman left him at a loss.

Ellie sucked in a deep breath, then swiped the tears from her eyes with both hands. "I'm sorry. Believe it or not, I never cry. You must think I'm a blithering mess."

"There's nothing for you to be sorry for. You're an amazing woman who's carrying a heavy load." He glanced around the parking lot, searching for bystanders who might have seen them arrive and witnessed her crying jag. Thank goodness, he didn't see any.

She sniffled and swiped her eyes once again, using the backs of both hands, but the tears continued to stream down her pretty face.

Steven had no idea what to say, but there was no way he'd just drop her off in the city parking lot like this and go on his own way. "Give me your address. I'm not going to let you drive home right now. I'll bring you back for your car later, when you're feeling better."

He expected an argument, a show of strength and determination, but she surprised him by saying, "Four eighteen Pumpernickel Court. It's a small subdivision near the elementary school. And you don't have to take me back to pick up my car. Daria should be home soon. I'll have her drop me off after dark. Or maybe even in the morning."

He nodded, then drove across town.

When he turned down the quiet, tree-lined street, Ellie said, "It's the white house with red-brick trim. The one with the big elm tree in the front yard."

Steven parked along the curb, then walked with her to the front porch and waited for her to unlock the door. She hadn't sent him on his way yet, and unless she did, he planned to stick around until her friend got home.

Ellie had no more than turned the key when a whine sounded from inside. "Tank must be home. I asked one of the neighbors to look after him while I was gone." She opened the door and stepped into a small, cozy living room as the scruffy black pup ran to her full throttle, nearly taking her out at the knees.

"Did you think we abandoned you, Tank?" She stooped to give the little mutt a scratch behind floppy ears.

When she straightened, Tank sat on his haunches and looked up at Steven, who stooped to greet him, too. "Hey there, little guy. Or should I say big guy? He's going to be a moose when he grows into those paws."

"I know. Right?" Ellie shut the door.

"He's not what I'd call cute," Steven said, "but he's friendly. There's something likable about him."

At that, for the first time since they'd left San Antonio, Ellie smiled, and his heart went out to her.

"We've been trying to housebreak him," Ellie said, "but he's still learning. Have a seat while I let him out in the backyard."

As the pup trailed after Ellie, Steven sat on the brown leather sofa and scanned the small living area, with its pale green walls and redbrick fireplace. A colorful area rug adorned hardwood floors.

Moments later, Ellie returned without Tank. "I'm sorry for falling apart at the seams."

"No problem."

She combed her fingers through her hair, then plopped down in a matching leather recliner. "I'm tired of hiding my pregnancy, although I can't do that much longer."

"Don't worry. People will adjust to the news. And life will go on."

"I know. You're right. But I've worked so hard to prove to some of my older and more conservative constituents that I'm a capable leader. I might be a young woman, but I want them to realize that my age and gender are assets, not liabilities."

"I agree completely," Steven said. "You're tough, but you also have heart." It was a nice combination.

"When the townspeople learn that I not only got involved with the wrong guy, but that I'm expecting his baby, they'll forget all the good I've done and focus on the mistakes. Not that I consider the baby a mistake. It's just that…" She blew out a ragged breath.

"You championed several big projects in the community," Steven said, "like the new park next to the lake. Thanks to you, Rambling Rose now has a beautiful greenbelt, and the children have a place to play. No one is going to forget that."

"Maybe not, but I don't want anything to jeopardize the work that still needs to be done." The long black strands, somewhat messy now from her meltdown, slid over her shoulder. *How could her ex-boyfriend just walk away from her?*

Steven sat quietly while she talked, mostly about being judged for having two X chromosomes and for being a millennial.

"You saw it today," she said. "Can you believe that those two women were so critical of me? You'd think they'd be happy to see one of their own take on a leadership position."

"They might be women," Steven said, "but they're nothing like you. They're clearly jealous. And they should be."

"Thanks, but now that they suspect I'm pregnant, they're going to spread the word. And then everyone will start asking questions I don't want to answer, especially about my personal life."

"Welcome to the world of politics," he said. "People are always going to have questions."

He'd do anything to help her, but there wasn't much he could do. Or was there?

She zeroed in on him with those big brown eyes, still a bit puffy, yet just as pretty as ever. "Don't you, Steven? Have questions, I mean?"

"Actually, I do. A lot of them. But I also have a suggestion." It elbowed itself front and center, then rolled right off his tongue. "Let's get married."

Chapter Nine

Ellie's jaw dropped. *Married?* He had to be kidding. "Don't make jokes."

"It's not a joke. The way I see it, if we were married, people wouldn't ask nosy questions."

"They'll also think the baby is yours."

He shrugged. "So what?" Then he laughed. "Hell, Ellie, having my baby might even bump up your poll numbers!"

At that, she rolled her eyes and frowned.

"Come on," he said. "Now, *that* was a joke."

She studied him for a couple of beats, then slowly shook her head. "We can't get married. We barely know each other. And after all the times we've bumped heads over one thing or another, who'd ever believe that we fell in love?"

"People who like to gossip, most likely. But you have to admit that marriage would solve at least part of your problem."

"And create a brand-new one."

"Nothing we couldn't fix together. After the baby is old enough, we can separate and get a quiet divorce."

Dang. He *was* serious. She tilted her head slightly, waiting for him to come to his senses. But he continued to sit there.

"What's in it for you?" she asked.

"Your friendship, I guess. I just want to help. Besides, it's not like either of us is dating anyone else right now."

"I don't know what to say. It sounds so…simple. Yet devious."

"It might be a sneaky ploy, but who would get hurt? The way I see it, you don't have too many options right now."

"So you're proposing a marriage of convenience?"

"If that's what you want to call it, sure. Why not?"

"Because there'd be nothing convenient about it." She studied him, expecting him to laugh off the sweet but ridiculous idea, but he didn't.

"Ellie, I just want to help."

She combed her fingers through her hair again, as if that might help her come to a decision. "It seems so…impulsive. Can I think about it?"

"Sure. But don't wait too long. I might get a better offer." She looked at him skeptically for a moment, and he laughed. "That was another joke."

"This isn't a laughing matter."

"No, it's not. But think it over. We can talk more about it in the morning."

Then he left her to ponder his offer. And that was exactly what she did. She stewed over the wacky proposal from the moment Steven walked out the front door until twenty minutes later, when her roommate and confidante came home.

Daria had no more than set down her purse when Ellie blurted out the latest twist in her current dilemma.

"Married? No kidding?" Daria asked. "He can't be serious."

"Those were my thoughts exactly. But he seems sincere."

"So talk to me." Daria plopped down on the sofa, taking the same cushion on which Steven had sat when he'd suggested the wild-ass solution to her problem. "I'm listening."

That was one of many things Ellie appreciated most about her best friend. Daria understood the way Ellie's mind worked, the way she talked out loud as she pondered a solution to a problem. And right now, she had a big one.

So Ellie chattered on, and Daria listened. When she finally took a break, her mind still reeling, Daria offered up an opinion. "It sounds to me as if Steven has fallen in love with you."

"Oh no. That's not it. We're just friends."

"Ellie." Daria blew out a sigh. "Friends tell me when I have a piece of spinach in my teeth. They listen to me complain about the jerk who claimed to be single and asked me out for drinks. Then, when he went to the restroom and spotted his wife, he left me sitting on a bar stool like a jilted fool."

True. Ellie and Daria had been through a lot together. "Friends also stand beside me while I puke my brains out each morning. And then they wipe my face with a damp cloth."

"That's right," Daria said. "And you're welcome. But friends don't offer to marry you just to save you from temporary embarrassment."

Ellie slunk back in her seat on the recliner, her hands on the armrests. "I know. But there's no way Steven is in love with me. He's just being nice. Besides, he said we'd get a quiet divorce after the baby gets here."

"I repeat," Daria said. "Friends don't offer to marry you. I'll bet you a nickel to a doughnut that Steven Fortune has fallen for you."

"That's impossible." Steven did care about her, though. And there was definitely some sexual attraction at play. He'd even kissed her. *Twice.* Of course, they'd been friendly kisses. Sort of. She'd been tempted to kiss him back, too. And if she had let loose the way she'd been tempted to, those kisses wouldn't have been so friendly.

That evening, Ellie continued to talk out her dilemma while Daria drove her to the city hall parking lot to pick up her car. And then again, after they got home and ate dinner.

By the time bedtime rolled around, Ellie had come to the conclusion that Steven had offered her an easy way out, and she'd be a fool not to take him up on it. But each time she decided to call him and tell him her decision, she'd go sideways.

How could she marry a man she didn't love?

Sure, she had feelings for Steven. What woman wouldn't? He was drop-dead gorgeous, smart and funny. But marriage was a big step. And so was a divorce.

Ellie prided herself on being an overachiever, a winner. And she'd hate for anyone to think she'd failed at holding a marriage together, even if it was fake.

Needless to say, by the time she arrived at city hall the next morning, she still hadn't touched base with Steven. How could she, when she didn't know what to tell him?

Doing her best to shake off her worries, she breezed into the lobby as if this were just another day in Rambling Rose.

"Good morning," Iris Tompkins, the receptionist, said. "The newspaper was delivered a few minutes ago. I put it on your desk."

"Thanks, Iris."

Before Ellie ran for mayor, her news source was either the internet or an app on her phone. But during the campaign, she'd begun reading a hard copy because she thought it gave her a better glimpse at the business world, especially when she looked at various ads. Besides, when she read the news off her phone, people at the coffee shop probably thought she was checking social media or playing a stupid game.

She'd no more than taken a seat behind her desk and started to flip through the pages when she spotted a write-up about the mayors' conference to promote tourism. She read it carefully, relieved that it didn't mention her name.

She continued to scan the newspaper for other articles, intending to skip the gossip page, but a photograph jumped out at her. No wonder that brunette at the conference had looked familiar. Her picture had to have been taken ten years ago—and had clearly been touched up—but she was the blasted columnist.

*What Texas politician and media darling's
recent weight gain has nothing to do with a
fondness for fast food and desserts? We won't
name names, but let's just say we expect the
truth to pop out any day now...*

Ellie's breath caught, and her gut clenched. The
gossip columnist hadn't mentioned her by name,
but it was pretty obvious. Her secret was out. She'd
better drive over to her parents' house and give
them the news in person before they heard it else-
where.

But did she dare take the time to do it now?

Since Steven and Ellie had agreed to talk in the
morning, he hadn't expected a call from her last
night, but it was a workday and already past ten
o'clock. Shouldn't he have heard something from
her by now?

He strode the length of modular office they'd
set up at the Paz job site, turned and walked back
again. When he realized he was pacing like a nervous fool, he swore under his breath and stopped.

Why in the hell was he anxious for an answer
to his proposal for a marriage that wasn't even
going to be real? It was nuts. Yet he looked at the
clock once again.

How long did it take a woman to make up her

mind? All she had to do was give him a one-word answer. A simple yes or no. How hard could that be?

Ellie might be a strong woman, but she feared telling her parents, which meant she had a chink in her armor, leaving her vulnerable. He'd seen the look on her face when that nasty brunette launched her attack. Were there other people out there who were eager to tarnish Ellie's reputation and ruin her political career?

Steven wasn't going to hang around waiting in the office all day, feeling like a caged animal, ready to snap at anyone who knocked at the door. He grabbed his keys off the desk and headed out the door, stopping long enough to tell the retiring office manager that he was going to be out of pocket for a while. Then he drove to city hall.

Once inside the lobby, he marched right past the receptionist, who tried to call him back. He ignored her and strode all the way back to Ellie's office. He probably ought to knock, but the door was ajar, so he pulled it open.

Ellie sat at her desk, her back to the doorway, the telephone receiver pressed to her ear.

"It's an invasion of privacy," she snapped, "and it's an example of low-life quasi journalism."

Steven took a repentant step back, planning to shut the door quietly and slip off without her noticing when her chair turned and he saw her expression and realized she was clearly disturbed, if not angry.

He assumed it was due to his unannounced arrival until her chair turned again and she spoke directly into the receiver. "I'm canceling my subscription, and you'd better hope that's all I do." Then she slammed down the phone, ending the call without saying goodbye.

"I'm sorry," he said. "I didn't mean to interrupt you. The door was open, but I should have knocked."

Ellie let out an unladylike sound and waved him in. Then she handed him the newspaper and pointed to an article in the gossip column.

After reading it, he realized why she'd called the paper to complain. "Who wrote that crap?"

"An anonymous junior reporter, I was told. But check out the picture of the columnist on the top. It was probably taken ten years or more ago and Photoshopped, but I know exactly who wrote it."

He did too. He recognized the woman in the photo. The rude, loudmouth brunette they'd seen in San Antonio.

"I'm sorry," he said.

"And I'm furious. I ought to make the official announcement and get it over with. But I'd hate to have a bad decision I made a year and a half ago dog me all over town."

He figured she was referring to the day she'd

met the father of her baby. "How long are you going to beat yourself up for misjudging someone's character?"

"As long as it takes."

He wasn't sure what she meant by that, but her frustration was evident when she combed her fingers through her hair, only to make a cute mess of the tidy topknot she wore in professional situations.

"I offered you a solution," he said. "Are you going to take me up on it?"

Ellie pushed her chair away from the desk, got to her feet and crossed her arms. "As much as I appreciate the kindness behind it, I can't marry you. I'm not going to saddle you with a wife and child."

"It would only be temporary. Besides, we're friends, right? You wouldn't be a burden."

"Don't you think marriage is a good way to ruin a friendship?"

"I won't let it," he said. "I give you my word."

She furrowed her brow—pondering his offer, he hoped.

"Ellie," he continued, "I really like you. And even when we bump heads about one thing or another, I respect you. Believe me when I say that I don't want to lose that. I give you my word, when this is all over, we'll still be friends—maybe even better ones than we are now."

"You make it sound so easy. But it's a wild and crazy solution." She slowly shook her head, but stopped abruptly. She blinked a couple of times. Her breath caught, and she paled. Then she placed both hands on her desk, bracing herself.

Steven hurried toward her, watching her sway, and reached her just as she crumpled against his side.

He glanced at the phone, prepared to hold her tight with one hand while dialing 9-1-1. The fire department was just down the street. It wouldn't take paramedics long to get here.

"Are you okay?" he asked, his heart pounding like a jackhammer at a construction site.

"I…feel a little…faint."

That was normal, right? Something pregnant women experienced all the time? Nothing to be concerned about?

He helped her take a seat. "Let me get you some water. Are you going to be okay if I leave you sitting there?"

"I'll be fine. I just got a little light-headed. That's all."

"No, that's not *all*. The stress is getting to be too much, and your body is rebelling. You've got to relieve some of the pressure, and I suggested a way for you to do that. Wait here. I'll be back."

Moments later, Steven returned with a disposable cup filled with water. He handed it to her, then knelt at her feet, watching until she drank half of it.

"Thanks." She managed a weak smile and set the cup on the desk.

"You're welcome. But just for the record, Ellie, I asked you a question. And I'm not going to take no for an answer."

She didn't respond right away, but by the look of resignation in her eyes, he could tell she was about to agree. That is, until she gazed at the open doorway and gasped. Her expression morphed into one of mortification.

Steven glanced over his shoulder and spotted an older Hispanic couple standing in the doorway, their brows furrowed, their eyes clearly troubled.

"Papa," Ellie said, her voice soft. "Mama."

Damn. What were her parents doing here? She clearly hadn't expected to see them. Had they read the gossip page in the newspaper and connected the dots?

Steven had no idea what thoughts were running through their minds, but he wasn't going to remain on his knees. He got to his feet, rose to his full height and said, "Mr. and Mrs. Hernandez. We haven't been formally introduced, but I'm Steven Fortune, one of the owners of Fortune Brothers Construction."

"I know who you are," Ellie's father said. "Most people in town do. And they're aware of the business you've brought to town. But they're not all happy about it."

Whether the older man was for or against the new businesses that had popped up, he didn't say. He merely looked Steven up and down, assessing him. Or maybe he was assessing the awkward situation he'd just walked in on—his daughter pale and uneasy, a man kneeling beside her.

"Ellie is an amazing woman," Steven said. "And she's a good mayor. The townspeople love her. You must be very proud of her."

Mr. Hernandez didn't speak, but his wife did. "Ellie has been nothing but a joy and a delight. She's been a real blessing to our family. We've always been proud."

"And up until today," Mr. Hernandez said, "she's never kept any secrets from us."

Steven glanced at Ellie, who appeared to be a little too overwhelmed to speak. And why wouldn't she be? First she'd read that shocking article, then she'd had the argument with the newspaper editor. She'd nearly fainted after that. And now her parents had arrived, their moods not difficult to discern.

"Mija," Mr. Hernandez said, "I can see what's going on in here."

"I know it looks a little odd, Papa, but I can explain. Steven stopped by city hall unexpectedly, and…" She looked first to Steven then back to her father, whose face had reddened to the point he might explode.

"Stopped by to *what*?" Mr. Hernandez asked. "Do all your constituents kneel at your feet, pressing you for an answer?"

She sucked in a deep breath. "Steven isn't just a constituent, Papa. He's my f—"

When she paused, Steven stepped in to help her out. "I'm her fiancé. I asked her to be my wife, and she agreed."

Chapter Ten

Ellie hadn't wanted to go along with Steven's scheme, but she'd just fallen into it. Now here she was, sitting behind the mayor's desk, nodding in agreement like a dumbstruck schoolgirl rather than a competent city leader.

"You're *engaged*?" Papa asked, his voice sharp, his brow furrowed. "And you haven't even introduced your mother and me to the man?"

Mama eased a step closer, her soft brown eyes wounded. "Why didn't you? Were you ashamed of us?"

"Oh God. No, Mama. I've never been ashamed of you! I never will be. It's just that…" Flustered,

Ellie shot a tight-lipped frown at Steven that all but said, *You and your big ideas. Now what?*

As if reading her thoughts, Steven placed his hand on her shoulder and gave it a gentle squeeze. "Ellie and I wanted to surprise you."

"When?" Papa remained in the doorway, his shoulders straight, his chest expanded, his expression a cross between anger and disappointment. "After the wedding?"

"Later today," Steven said.

Papa shot Steven a look of disapproval. "My wife and I don't run in the same wealthy, highfalutin social circles as you, so I don't know how you people handle things. But in my family, in my culture, a man is expected to approach a young woman's father first and ask for his blessing."

"I'm sorry, sir. You're right. I should have done that." The contrite expression Steven wore was one Ellie hadn't seen before. She rather liked it today, especially since his crazy idea had just blown up in his face. Hers, too. Yet at the same time, sympathy fluttered in her heart and up to her throat.

"Steven planned to ask for my hand, Papa. But things happened rather quickly. I'm afraid it's a little complicated."

Papa nodded at her desk, where the newspaper lay open to the gossip column. "I can see how things got complicated."

Guilt warmed Ellie's cheeks. Her parents had

read the morning paper and then they'd marched right over to city hall to ask her if it was true.

"Are you really expecting a baby?" Mama asked.

Ellie tried to hold her head up while kicking herself for not telling them sooner. "Yes, it's true. I'm so sorry you had to find out like this."

"When were you going to tell us?" Mama asked, her eyes watering.

Soon. Maybe tonight. But before Ellie could respond, Iris, the lobby receptionist, peered around her father's back and said, "Excuse me. I don't mean to interrupt."

Ellie cringed. How long had she been standing there? How much had she heard? "What do you need, Iris?"

"I wanted to remind you of that meeting at the water district this morning. It's at eleven."

Ellie didn't forget meetings, although that one might have slipped her mind today. "Thanks. I didn't forget. It's on my calendar."

Iris scanned Ellie's office, taking in the three people who stood in the room while Ellie sat at her desk. "Is everything okay?"

Heck no. Ellie's fairy-tale life had taken another hit. A big one. And she didn't want the Rambling Rose rumor mill getting wind of it. "Everything is fine, Iris. Please close the door on your way out."

The friendly—sometimes overly so—receptionist took a step back. "Oh. Of course."

When the office door snapped shut, Steven cleared his throat. "Mr. and Mrs. Hernandez, this is partially my fault."

Papa chuffed. *"Partially?"*

Undaunted, Steven continued. "Ellie wanted to tell me about the baby before she told you, but we hadn't been dating very long. We'd also kept it on the down low for political reasons. And even though we had strong feelings for each other, she wasn't sure how I'd feel about her pregnancy—or how she wanted to break the news to me. So she's been dragging her feet."

"How *do* you feel about it?" Mama asked him.

"I'll admit, the baby took us both a little by surprise. But I'm happy. We both are. In fact, I got on bended knee and proposed just before you two arrived."

Mama looked first at Ellie, then at Steven. "Have you set a date?"

"Not yet," Steven said, "but under the circumstances, I don't think we should wait very long."

"The sooner the better, I'd say." Papa raked a hand through his thinning gray hair.

"A wedding takes time to plan." Mama took another step into the room. "You'll need a dress. And invitations will need to be ordered. Then there are the flowers. Cake tastings. It can get expensive, *mija*. But don't worry. We've been setting money aside to pay for your wedding, just like we did for college. It's there for you now."

Another pang of guilt struck Ellie. Her parents had been saving and going without vacations, new cars and God only knew what else to provide for what they assumed would be a special day. "Thank you, Mama. I promise not to use it all. It's going to be a small wedding. Just family and a few close friends."

Papa chuffed. "The Fortune family alone will take up the entire church."

Mama had softened and gotten on board, but Papa was clearly not happy and still had a long way to go. If this was his reaction to a fiancé on one knee, how would he have reacted if she'd faced him without a husband in sight and told him she was pregnant?

"Will you let me help you plan it?" Mama asked.

"Of course. I'd love that. Daria is going to be my maid of honor. So the three of us can plot and shop together. It'll be fun."

Mama's sweet smile offset the tension in the room. "I can't wait. I've been dreaming of this day for a long time. I've also dreamed of holding a grandbaby in my arms. When is it due? Have you seen a doctor yet?"

Ellie smiled, happy to have her mother's full support. "The baby is due in mid-August, and the doctor said everything is going well. I have another appointment next week. Would you like to go with me?"

"I'd *love* that!" Mama turned to Papa, her eyes watery but bright. "*Mi amor*. We're going to be *abuelitos*. Isn't that wonderful?"

Papa let out a humph, announcing that he wasn't as delighted as Mama. At least, not now. He could be tough at times, but he had a good heart.

"I can't wait to tell my bunco group," Mama said. "They'll want to throw a shower for you. Actually, two of them. One for the wedding and then for the baby."

Ellie looked at Steven, wishing they could speak telepathically. If they could, she'd tell him that his solution to her problem had gotten way out of hand. And now she felt like Sandra Bullock onboard that runaway bus with Keanu Reeves. She just hoped that the two of them would end up living through it all and saving the other unwitting passengers.

Like Keanu, Steven might be a gorgeous, sexy hunk. But that didn't mean he could help her save the day. They'd have to talk more later, when they were alone and could put their heads together to slow the bus and steer it in a better direction.

"Mama," Ellie said, "for political reasons, I'm not ready for the news to leak out until I have a solid game plan in place. So would you and Papa please keep it to yourselves for a few days?"

"Of course, although it's going to be hard to keep quiet. It's all so exciting."

Papa didn't look too excited, but hopefully, after Mama worked on him and he had a chance to cool down, he'd come around.

"By the way," Ellie said, "you didn't ask, but I found out two weeks ago that the baby is a boy."

Mama lifted her hands to her face, placed them together as if in prayer, then she gave a muffled little clap and turned to Papa. "Did you hear that, George? We're having a grandson. Now you'll have someone to take fishing. Maybe he'll help you fix up that old car you've been storing in the garage."

Papa had wanted to restore that 1973 Bronco for ages, but since he couldn't seem to tell his boss at the auto repair shop that he was going to retire, Mama had feared it would sit there for years.

Ellie got up from the desk chair, slowly and carefully so she wouldn't risk getting light-headed again. Then she crossed the office to embrace each of her parents. "I love you both so much. I hope I haven't disappointed you too badly."

"We were a little taken aback at first," Mama said. "But we're not disappointed. Are we, George?"

Papa offered up a smile. "No, Ellie. You've always made us proud." Then he turned and eyed

Steven carefully. "You're the one who'd better not disappoint me, young man."

"I won't, sir."

Steven's lie didn't sit well with Ellie. When the time came for them to announce their divorce, Papa wouldn't be pleased at all.

She glanced at the clock on the wall. "I hate to rush everyone off, but I have a meeting at eleven. Can we talk more about this later?"

"Yes, of course." Mama kissed Ellie's cheek. "Call me tonight after you talk to Daria. Then we can plan our first shopping trip."

"I'll do that."

"Mr. Hernandez," Steven said, drawing her father's attention. He extended his arm, and Papa, thankfully, took his hand to shake. "You've raised a fine daughter, and we both have the utmost respect for you. When the baby gets here, we're going to name him George."

Papa blinked back his surprise. Or was it a tear welling his eye? "That would…" He cleared his throat. "That'd be… Well, I'm honored."

Ellie had known her father wouldn't stay angry very long, and he seemed to be feeling better about the situation already, which was a huge relief. At least the hardest part of the announcement had been made. And tomorrow morning, she'd call a press conference and ask Steven to stand beside her.

His phony marriage plan wasn't going to work out in the long run, but they were too deep into the pretense to change course now. Still, she wasn't looking forward to facing the community.

George and Alma Hernandez weren't the only Rambling Rose residents who read the San Antonio newspaper, and not all of them were on Team Fortune. At Mariana's Market, Jackson had implied that Ellie was a traitor for fraternizing with the Fortunes. So news of their upcoming marriage might not go over very well. And when everyone learned she was pregnant, they'd conclude that she'd actually slept with the enemy, even though she and Steven had barely kissed.

On the upside, Ellie always had been able to charm the press, as well as the community at large. So she wasn't overly worried, especially if Steven was at her side.

If he could handle Papa, the rest of the town would be a piece of cake.

After Ellie hurried to her meeting at the water district, Steven left city hall and returned to his office at Fortune Brothers Construction, where he spent the afternoon going over spreadsheets and blueprints, meeting with the accountant, and then taking part in several lengthy conference calls.

Finally, at a quarter to six, he called it a day, locked his office door and headed to his SUV.

He'd barely reached the parking lot when a tall, lanky reporter and a short, squat photographer rushed toward him.

"Is there any truth to the rumor that you asked Mayor Hernandez to marry you?" the reporter asked.

Oh, for Pete's sake. He'd known that word of his and Ellie's engagement would get out, but he hadn't expected it to happen so quickly. "No comment."

The camera flashed.

As Steven continued toward his vehicle without missing a beat, the reporter tried to match his strides. "Mr. Fortune, have the two of you set a date for the wedding?"

Ignoring the men and that blasted camera, Steven climbed into the SUV and drove away, his grip tight on the wheel. He'd like to throttle that damned gossip columnist. This was all her fault.

Ellie ought to sue the newspaper for printing that woman's salacious words, although the case would probably get thrown out based on a technicality. The columnist hadn't actually mentioned Ellie by name.

He suspected that Iris, the city hall receptionist, had contributed to the spread of gossip. She'd been curious when Steven had breezed past her on his way to Ellie's office this morning. And when George and Alma arrived with troubled expressions, her interest had probably been piqued, so she'd followed them.

She'd claimed to be standing outside the doorway so she could remind Ellie of a meeting, but Steven didn't buy that lame excuse. And now the Rambling Rose rumor mill was running amok.

If the newshounds were bothering him, he couldn't imagine what Ellie must be dealing with, so he called her cell.

She answered on the second ring.

"How's it going?" he asked.

"It's been a rough day, to say the least. That blasted gossip columnist has been stalking me. And apparently, there's a reporter camped in front of my house, too. Daria told me to stay away until he leaves, but he's not going anywhere until he get some answers."

"You're right. They're not just after you. When I left the office, a reporter and a photographer tried to corner me."

"This is getting out of hand," Ellie said. "We need to talk and work out a game plan."

"Where are you?" he asked.

"In my car. I was going to spend the night with my parents, but my mom told me there are a couple of local bloggers parked in front of their house. Apparently, the fact that a small town mayor is going to marry into the Fortune family has set off local interest. So I've been driving around town until I figure out where I can have some privacy."

"Come to the ranch. It's not only remote and a little difficult to find, we also have security. No one can get in the front gate without us knowing about it."

"Is your family okay with that? I mean, do they know what's going on?"

"Not yet, but they will. I'm going to call them now and give them a heads-up."

Ellie sighed. "This thing is snowballing on us, Steven."

True. They'd have to do some fast thinking. "Don't worry, Ellie. It'll be okay. We'll work it out."

"I hope you're right."

To be completely honest, so did Steven. But he'd always been able to think himself out of a corner.

"I have a guest bedroom," he said. "You should stay with me until we get everything figured out."

Silence stretched across the line for several pensive beats. Finally, she said, "Okay. I'll see you shortly."

With Ellie on her way to the ranch, Steven called Callum and briefed him on the upcoming wedding, as well as the nosy press. He'd expected his brother to be surprised, but he seemed to take the announcement in stride.

"I realize things came together pretty quickly," Steven said, "but don't worry. I know what I'm doing."

"It didn't take me long to fall for Becky," Callum said. "And we all saw the sparks between you and Ellie."

Sure, there was chemistry, along with physical attraction. But they'd bumped heads since day one for political reasons. Even their arguments and disagreements were passionate, in the broadest sense of the word.

Ignoring his brother and the suggestion he didn't want to deal with tonight, Steven said, "Ellie's right behind me. She's going to be staying with me."

"I'll let Becky and Dillon know."

Ten minutes later, Steven arrived at the gatehouse, where he greeted Stan Hawthorne, the guard.

"I've invited Ellie Hernandez up to the house again tonight. She's a few minutes behind me. There might be some snoopy reporters on her tail, but don't let them through."

"They won't get past me, Mr. Fortune."

Steven thanked him and drove up to the house. He hadn't told Callum everything. So, for all the family knew, the marriage would be the real deal, and they'd assume that Ellie would be sharing his bed. Instead, she'd sleep in his guest room, just across the hall.

The sleeping arrangements could prove to be a challenge, though. Their chemistry was strong. Hopefully, unlike the news of their engagement, his attraction to Ellie wouldn't get out of hand.

After parking next to the expansive main house at the Fame and Fortune Ranch, Ellie popped open her trunk to get the spare outfit and toiletries she carried with her for emergencies. A change of clothing and makeup had come in handy on more occasions than one, but she'd never been so glad to be prepared for the unexpected as she was today.

She removed the canvas gym bag she used for yoga and her aerobics class, as well as a garment bag that held another outfit. She had enough to get her through the night and the next day. Daria had promised to pack a suitcase tomorrow and bring it to the ranch.

Hopefully, she wouldn't need to be here long. Once the news was out, the reporters and bloggers would back off, she could go back to her house and life would go back to normal. Only trouble was, with a fake wedding and a baby on the way, her life was changing at Mach speed. And she was going to have a new normal, whatever that might be.

When she reached the front entrance, she shuffled the bags she carried, giving herself a free hand to ring the bell, but she didn't need to. The door swung open, and Steven greeted her with a warm smile that lit his blue eyes.

"Here," he said, reaching for her tote bag. "Let me carry that."

"Thank you." She stepped into the large foyer that opened to a formal living room, but rather than scan her surroundings, she studied the man who'd offered her refuge.

His hair was still damp from a recent shower, and the clean and musky scent of soap and man filled her lungs. He'd shed the Western wear he'd had on earlier, replacing them with a casual look—a black T-shirt and a pair of worn jeans. He'd kicked off his shoes, too.

She tore her gaze from the gorgeous sight and scanned the empty room. "Where is everyone?"

"I told them you'd had a rough day and that we needed some privacy tonight."

She hated to admit it, but she really would appreciate some peace and quiet.

"I don't want you passing out on me again," Steven added.

"I didn't pass out. Not all the way."

"Close enough to worry me." Steven nodded toward the hall that led to his quarters. "Come with me."

"I would like to have some quiet time," she

said, as she followed him down the hall, "but I feel bad about chasing everyone off."

"You didn't. Dillon's busy working on a project in his quarters, and since the twins didn't get a good nap today, Callum and Becky are getting them ready for bed." Steven stopped and opened the door for her. "If it makes you feel better, Becky told Manny, the cook and caretaker, that he could sleep in tomorrow morning. She wants to fix breakfast for us. That is, if you don't mind."

"No, that's fine. We'll need to face them together soon, and we may as well get it over with." Ellie entered Steven's small living room, with its leather furniture and southwestern artwork on the pale green walls.

"You didn't see the guest room when you were here last," he said. "It's across the hall from me." Steven led her to the room in which she'd be sleeping and placed her bag on a queen-size bed covered with a white goose-down comforter. She would've found it to be cozy and restful if Steven hadn't been standing so close, if his warm gaze and blood-stirring scent weren't so alluring.

"Do you want to take a rest before dinner?" he asked.

"Actually, if you don't mind, I think I'll take a shower and put on something more casual."

"No problem. I hope you don't mind sharing a bathroom with me."

"I'm just glad to have a peaceful place to stay tonight."

"It might be a little steamy in there, but I left clean towels on the counter. Let me know if you need anything."

"Thanks, but I have everything I'll need." She pointed to the bag on the bed. "I came prepared."

"I can see that." He offered her a heart-strumming smile, then left her on her own.

Twenty minutes later, she came out of the bathroom clean and refreshed. She wore black yoga pants and a white T-shirt, which she'd have to wear to bed tonight. Her emergency preparedness kit didn't cover sleepovers. She left her sneakers in the gym bag, opting to go barefoot.

She padded down the hall and found Steven in the kitchen, chopping lettuce for a salad.

He turned and smiled as his gaze swept over her from head to toe. "I've never seen you without shoes. Pretty toes."

Her cheeks flushed, embarrassed by the compliment, by the intimacy of their new living arrangement, but she stood tall. "I can dress casually when I want to."

"I'm glad you did."

He'd kicked back for the evening, too, and if anything, the barefoot cowboy was even more appealing that way. And sexier than ever.

"What's for dinner?" she asked.

"Nothing fancy. Just turkey sandwiches, a tossed salad and chips. I hope that's okay."

"That's fine." In fact, it was perfect. He was perfect. And the friend she'd come to appreciate more than she'd ever expected. "Need some help?"

"Nope. I got it all under control. I thought we'd eat indoors tonight. The sandwiches are made, and the salad is almost done. It'll just be a minute." Steven turned back to add cherry tomatoes to the greens.

Ellie pulled out one of two bar stools, then glanced out onto the patio and into the backyard. The same small white lights twinkled on the trees outside, and yet again she couldn't help but think how the whole scene appeared to be more romantic than it should.

"I've been thinking about the wedding," he said. "We need to set a date, and the sooner the better. What about next Sunday?"

Talk about soon! But he was right. She sighed. "All right. That'll work. But there's so much to do. Where do you suggest we have it?"

"Let's have it here. There's bound to be a few newshounds trying to crash the ceremony, and we can easily step up the security. I'll just add a second guard at the gate that day."

He had a point. A good one.

"There's a large grassy area behind the main

house," he added. "We can rent chairs and a gazebo. It's up to you, though."

"That would be a nice touch, I guess. But I don't want the guest list to get out of hand."

"I can keep my number at a dozen or so," Steven said. "My parents will want to be here, and I'm sure Wiley, Ashley, Megan and Nicole will come with them. Then there's my sister Stephanie and her fiancé, Acton Donovan. And, of course, Dillon, Callum and Becky."

"There aren't too many people I'd need to include. My parents have a lot of friends and coworkers, not to mention my mom's bunco group, but I'll insist that we keep it a family affair. And, of course, Daria. She's like a sister to me."

"And she'll be the maid of honor." Steven reached for a pair of tongs and placed them in the salad bowl.

"Who will you ask to stand up with you?" Ellie asked.

Steven set the bowl on the bar, between the two stools. "If I go with one of my brothers, it would be a hard choice to make. I might ask my dad."

"That's kind of cool."

"I think so. I don't have a favorite brother, although I do have only one father."

Steven set two place mats on the bar, as well as silverware and a couple of napkins. He then took a bottle of water from the fridge and filled two glasses.

"Have you set up a shopping trip yet?"

"I would have done that this evening, but when I was talking to both my mom and Daria, we'd been more focused on avoiding the snoopy reporters. But I'll call the office and let them know I'm taking a few days off work. Hopefully, we can go shopping tomorrow."

"There's a store that sells formal wear at the Shoppes. It'd be nice if you can find a dress there."

To support the store owner, she assumed. And it was a nice thought. "I'd do it, but I don't think I'd be able to afford anything there."

He circled the edge of the bar to take his seat next to her, but he paused for a moment, just inches away, his eyes locked on hers. "Consider the dress my treat."

The offer, as well as the way he was looking at her, sent her senses reeling and her thoughts scampering to keep up. "Stop trying to be so nice."

"Can't help it." He grinned, then winked. "I *am* nice. You'll see."

They remained like that for a moment, bonded by an invisible tie, gazes locked, her heart thumping.

He reached out and cupped her jaw. His thumb skimmed her cheek, caressing her skin. She should stop him, push him away, jump out of her chair and run for the hills. But for the life of her, she couldn't move. As his lips brushed hers, she leaned into him and kissed him back.

His tongue swept into her mouth, and a wave of desire nearly knocked her to the floor. This was not good—the kiss, the desire for more, their current living situation.

Ellie let the heated kiss continue until her brain finally took control over her body, and she drew back. "I'm sorry, Steven. This isn't a good idea. We can't let it happen again."

He raked a hand through his hair, sucked in a deep breath, then slowly let it out. "You're probably right."

Then he winked at her again. "But you have to admit, it was nice."

It had been better than nice. And if things were different, she might be tempted to kiss him again, right here, right now. But the last thing she needed to do was fall for her fake fiancé.

And something told her she was getting too damned close to doing just that.

Chapter Eleven

The next morning, after Ellie dressed for the day and while she was making the bed in the guest room, Steven's deep, mesmerizing voice sounded from the open doorway.

"Becky and Callum made breakfast. Are you hungry?"

She placed the last pillow sham on the bed then turned to the door. "Yes, but I'm a little nervous about facing the troops. What, *exactly*, did you tell them about us?"

"Just that we'd been seeing each other for a while and that we tried to stay under the community's radar. Things got serious, and I asked you to marry me. You agreed, and now the press is hounding us."

"Okay. Got it." They'd touched upon that subject last night, but after they'd kissed, she'd gotten uneasy and made a quick retreat. But it was a new day now. She couldn't very well avoid the issue any longer. Nor could she avoid facing Steven's family.

"Is it okay to tell them about the baby?" he asked.

"We may as well." She rested her hand on her growing belly. "In fact, we really should."

Steven leaned a shoulder against the doorjamb. He'd never looked so handsome, so relaxed, so...

The memory of last night's kiss ricocheted in her mind. Try as she might, she couldn't seem to shake the blood-stirring yearning it provoked, the desire for more.

"I like seeing you do that," Steven said.

She took a step away from the bed, which was now made and a little too inviting, and eased closer to the doorway. It might be time to make another quick exit. "See me do what?"

"Rubbing your stomach like that. Caressing the baby."

The sweet sentiment, along with the appreciative way he studied her, darn near sucked the air from her lungs.

He lifted his hand toward her tummy. "Do you mind...?"

She didn't mind, but the question came as such a surprise that she could hardly speak. When she nodded, he leaned forward, placed a splayed hand on her baby bump and gave it a gentle, almost reverent stroke. Then he withdrew it and shrugged a single shoulder. "I'm sorry. I was…curious. I've never—"

"No," she said, her voice whisper soft, as she placed her own hand where his had been. "It's okay. I understand."

"This might sound lame, but I like seeing the maternal side of you. It adds a whole new dimension to the strong woman I've come to know and admire."

His sincerity, his praise, warmed her heart.

"Just so you know," he said, "I didn't mean to make you feel uncomfortable last night—when I kissed you."

The kiss itself hadn't made her uncomfortable. It was the feelings it stirred up, feelings that had been much too real for a fake engagement. "I got a little uneasy afterward, but it was nice while it was happening."

His head tilted slightly. "It was only *nice*?"

She crossed her arms and shifted her weight to one hip. "That's how you described it."

"I wasn't being entirely honest." He tossed her a playful grin that could easily turn her brain to mush again—if she'd let it. But that kiss had been too hot for comfort.

She couldn't remain in the same small room with the sexy man, close enough to breathe in his woodsy scent, and only a few steps from the bed. "This isn't going to work."

"What isn't?"

"Kissing. Touching. Pretending that we're romantically involved."

"Don't you think people will expect us to be affectionate?"

"In public? Probably. But being affectionate when we're behind closed doors will only make it seem real. And with a divorce on the horizon, we shouldn't complicate things. Right?"

"Good point."

"So you're not going to press for more kissing or touching or…anything more?"

He held up his hand in Boy Scout fashion. "I promise."

"Good." She'd won that round, although she didn't get the usual satisfaction she could expect when coming out on top of a deal. "I'm hungry. Come on. Let's go face the troops."

Steven followed her out of the room. When they reached the foyer, they walked side by side to the large, functional kitchen with state-of-the-art appliances and black marble counters. The warm aroma of breakfast filled the room, providing tantalizing whiffs of fresh-brewed coffee and bacon.

Two adorable toddlers sat in their high chairs, each of them with a sippy cup in hand. Callum stood beside them, placing chunks of banana on their trays, while Becky operated the griddle on the stove, flipping hotcakes.

Ellie had met Callum's future wife a couple of times, but only at ribbon-cutting ceremonies. They really hadn't talked very much, but Ellie found the brunette with sparkling brown eyes to be sweet and likable—nice qualities for a nurse.

"Good morning," Steven said from the doorway.

Becky turned and blessed them both with a warm smile. "Breakfast is almost ready. Can I get you a cup of coffee, Ellie? We have orange juice, too."

"OJ sounds good," Ellie said. "Thank you."

"Where's Dillon?" Steven asked Callum.

"He cut out early. Said he had to meet with one of the suppliers in town."

Steven strode to the cupboard, pulled out a white mug and poured his own coffee. "Ellie and I had a chance to talk a little more last night. We decided to get married at the ranch on Sunday. Nothing big or fancy. Just a small, private ceremony."

One of the twins slapped her hand down on the tray, mashing a banana chunk in the process, and squealed with glee at the goo on her hand. Her sister grinned and smashed one of her own.

Steven laughed at the messy antics.

"Hey, bro," Callum said, "wait until you have a toddler or two. You might not find their messes so funny."

"I won't have to wait long for that," Steven said. "Ellie's having a baby in August."

At that, Callum's gaze dropped to Ellie's belly, then he cut a furrowed-brow look at Steven. "Your wedding announcement didn't surprise me a bit, but I didn't see *that* coming. Now I can see why you're in a hurry to tie the knot."

"What he means," Becky said, "is that we couldn't be happier for you two—the wedding, the baby and the whole nine yards. Welcome to the family, Ellie."

"She's absolutely right," Callum said. "It's a happy surprise."

"If there's anything I can do," Becky added, "whether it's to help you settle in at the ranch or get ready for the wedding, just let know."

"Thanks." Ellie's cheeks warmed at Becky's kindness, at her obvious acceptance. "I appreciate that."

While the two precious toddlers sat in their high chairs, making quite the mess of their meal, the adults took their seats at the large kitchen table and ate their fill of blueberry pancakes, scrambled eggs and turkey bacon.

Becky chatted about the pleasures of pregnancy and the joys of childbirth, her words more enlightening because of her medical background. She couldn't have been sweeter or more accepting.

Yet the more kindness the couple showed to her, the guiltier Ellie felt. She hated deceiving people who'd welcomed her into their home and family with open arms. But she had to continue to keep up the pretense.

She and Steven were in too deep to do otherwise.

Ellie had made it plain to Steven that she intended their relationship to remain platonic, although he wasn't so sure her hormones agreed with her. His certainly didn't.

He had no intention of breaking his promise not to push for more, but it was killing him. And so were the cold showers.

For the past couple of nights, climbing into bed alone and knowing that Ellie slept just across the hall had been a hell of a lot harder for him to handle than he'd expected. The woman grew prettier and sexier each time he laid eyes on her. And since she'd decided to work remotely, he saw her daily.

He tried to avoid her by spending more time on the jobsite or at the office, but that didn't help. Not when he constantly envisioned her back at the ranch, wandering through his quarters, barefoot, her long hair hanging loose and glossy over her shoulders and down her back. What guy wouldn't be distracted?

And then there was the wedding talk and all the chores. Ellie had sent out a press release two days ago, announcing their engagement and upcoming marriage without providing any details. Then she'd slipped off the property to meet her mom and Daria, who'd taken her to shop in San Antonio so they could avoid the rumor mill in Rambling Rose. Fortunately, they found a dress and ordered the flowers that afternoon.

Steven didn't ask to be included in the shopping trips, but he insisted on taking part in the cake tasting that Picard's Patisserie hosted at the ranch.

Picard outdid himself with the samples he set out on the table in the main kitchen. Then the short, balding baker proudly stood by as Steven, Ellie, Alma, Daria and Becky studied the miniature cakes he'd placed in front of them.

"What's this?" Steven pointed to the most decadent sample.

"That's the Black Forest," Picard said. "It's a chocolate cake with kirsch, whipped cream and topped with tart cherries."

"And this one?" Ellie asked.

"It's a white cake with Grand Marnier flavor and a raspberry buttercream filling."

After a couple of bites, the ladies began to rave about Picard and his cakes, much to the delight of the French baker. Steven wondered if they'd be able to settle on a favorite. At least, until he tasted the last sample in front of him.

"Ellie." He reached for her fork, cut into the small cake and offered her a bite. "Try this."

She opened her mouth, and he gave her a taste. Her eyes lit up. "Oh, yes. This one. I love it."

As she licked the frosting from her lips, Steven forgot about the almond-flavored cake with a filling that tasted like crème brûlée.

All he cared about was Ellie, and getting a sweet taste of her.

The other women quickly agreed that they'd chosen the perfect cake.

Picard happily took the order and promised to deliver it himself on Sunday morning, prior to the ceremony that afternoon.

As far as Steven knew, everything was set. They'd only invited immediate family and a few close friends, but with a few extra additions made here and there, Steven had to call the party-rental people to increase the number of chairs they'd need to deliver.

In the meantime, he'd done a little shopping of his own at his favorite Western-wear shop, picking up a black jacket and slacks as well as a fancy white shirt.

An hour ago, he'd left the office early to pick up his jacket from the tailor. He'd considered going back to work but decided to call it a day and went home instead. Ellie had been spending a lot of time in seclusion, having taken some days off from city hall, and deserved to go out to dinner for a change. So he decided to surprise her.

He entered his living quarters and, finding them quiet and empty, assumed Ellie was with Becky on the other side of the house. So he went to the bedroom, hung his jacket in the closet and kicked off his boots. He'd no more than stepped back into the hallway when the bathroom door opened, and Ellie walked out wrapped in a fluffy white towel.

She gasped and nearly jumped out of her skin. "Oh my gosh. *Steven.* You scared me."

And she mesmerized him. Whether dressed in business attire or rocking a pair of jeans, Ellie Hernandez was a beautiful woman. But wearing only a towel? He couldn't find words to describe her.

"I'm sorry," he said. "I didn't mean to frighten you."

"That's okay. I just didn't expect you. I mean, this is your house." She pointed at the open door to her room, nearly losing her grip on the towel in the process. "I forgot to bring a change of clothes into the bathroom with me..." She studied him for a moment, nearly as closely as he watched her.

"You're making me crazy," he said. And if she dropped the towel, he'd be toast.

She'd told him twice that she was conflicted about kissing or getting too close, even if her body language was giving him a much different spin. Only a jerk would push her now, no matter how badly he wanted to.

"It's not that I don't want to," she added.

"I know. I do, too. But I get it." The political stuff had gotten in the way.

For a moment, a sense of apprehension settled over him. Would making love hurt either of them in the long run?

How could it? They were both going into the fake marriage knowing that it had an ending date. As long as they both kept that in mind, everything would be fine.

Steven might have repeated the rules, but he wasn't a jerk. If they were going to make love, Ellie would have to make the first move, which she apparently was reluctant to do.

He was about to retreat to his bedroom, the living area or even to the stable when she eased toward him.

Was she changing her mind about getting in too deep? He hoped to hell that's what was happening, but he'd made her a promise. And he'd be damned if he'd break it.

She continued to close the gap between them. "This is crazy, Steven."

Yes, it was. The tall, willowy brunette, her dark brown eyes doe-like, was making him nuts. And so was her springtime scent as it burrowed deep in his nostrils, making a memory.

"We're not supposed to do this."

"If it makes you feel better," he said, "everyone already thinks we're lovers. And we'll be married on Sunday afternoon."

"I know, but making love will only complicate things."

"Maybe so." But if she was game, he was. "Our engagement might be fake, but the chemistry between us is the real deal. I don't know about you, but a cold shower isn't going to help me this time."

"Damn you, Steven."

Her lips parted, and he cupped her jaw, his fingers extending to her neck, her hair draping over his knuckles. "Say the word, Ellie, and I'll walk away."

When she didn't raise an objection, he kissed her, deeply and thoroughly, sending a rush of heat through his veins, his blood pounding in need. She swayed slightly then reached for his shoulder to keep her balance.

He didn't feel all that steady himself, so he scooped her into his arms and carried her to his bed, where he laid her down, her long black hair splayed upon the pillow sham, her beautiful body stretched out on top of the matching comforter.

He paused for a beat, drinking in the angelic sight, until a shadow of insecurity crossed her brow.

She placed a hand on her belly and worried her bottom lip. "I'm not usually this...round."

"Don't say that, Ellie. Don't even think it. You're the prettiest, sexiest expectant mother I've ever seen."

She clicked her tongue and all but rolled her eyes. "Oh, come on, Steven. How many pregnant women have you seen naked?"

"Just you. And believe me, I like what I see." He nodded at the bed where she lay. "Do you mind...?"

She rolled to the side, making room for him. And that was the only encouragement he needed. He removed his clothes. All the while, she watched him with passion-glazed eyes—as eager as he was, it seemed, to feel his skin against hers.

With a straining erection evidence of his arousal, he slowly joined her on the bed. Yet as eager as he was to make love with her, he wanted to take it slow and easy, taking his time to please her—and to ensure he didn't do anything that might hurt the baby.

He placed a gentle hand on her belly. "I'll be careful."

"I know you will, but don't worry. You won't hurt me or the baby."

He kissed her again—long and deep. As their bodies pressed together, their hands stroked, caressed, explored until they were both caught up in the throes of passion. His only thought, his only concern was to please her the way she was pleasing him.

His thumb skimmed across her taut nipple, and when her breath caught, he bent his head and took the sweet tip into his mouth, tonguing it, sucking it, until she gripped his shoulders, sending a rush of heat pounding through his blood.

He couldn't seem to get enough of her. Looking. Touching. Tasting. He stroked her skin, so soft. And he studied the flecks of gold in her eyes, saw the desire brewing there. He spotted something else, too. Emotions he'd never seen, never sensed, churned in her gaze. It ought to scare the hell out of him, but it intrigued him, drew him in.

"I hope I'm not sorry about this later," she said, yet her grip on his shoulder didn't ease.

"You won't be," he said. "I'll make sure there's nothing to regret."

He brushed his lips across her brow, holding back, allowing her to change her mind, although it would probably kill him if she did.

"I want you," Ellie said, her voice barely a whisper as she cupped his face with both hands. "I need to feel you inside me."

He didn't want to prolong the foreplay any longer, either. He entered her slowly at first, getting the feel of her, the feel of them. Her body responded to his, and she arched up to meet each of his thrusts. In and out. Taking and giving.

Should he slow the pace, take it a little easier?

Her breath caught, and she gripped his shoulders, her nails pressing into his skin. "Yes. Oh, yes..."

That was all he needed to hear. He increased the tempo until she reached a peak, crying out with her climax and sending him over the edge. He let go, shuddering as he released with her in a sexual explosion that had him seeing stars spinning in the night sky.

He held her close, relishing each wave of pleasure, too overcome to speak. He'd known making love with her would be amazing, but he hadn't expected it to be quite like this.

They'd forged a bond, it seemed, one that most friends never had. And while he meant to keep his promise to her, that he wouldn't let them get in too deep, he had to admit that sex had never felt so good, so right.

The scent of their lovemaking swirled around them as he relished the sweet afterglow. When his heart rate finally began to slow to a normal pace, he rolled to the side, taking her with him. He brushed a strand of hair from her brow and looked down at her.

She smiled leisurely, and he kissed the tip of her nose. "Who would've ever thought that being friends with benefits would be as incredible as this?" he said.

She flinched, then slowly eased out of his embrace.

"What's wrong?" he asked.

"Nothing. Not really. It was definitely good. I just wish we wouldn't have acted on our impulses. There's too much at stake, and I don't want to screw up our friendship."

Then she rolled to the side, grabbed her towel and headed out of the room, messing with his pride and leaving him more than a little bewildered.

Ellie returned to the guest room, snatched the clothes she'd left on the bed and went to the bathroom to freshen up and get dressed. All the while, she kicked herself for being so impulsive.

She was a bright, capable woman who always weighed the options and thought things through. But not today. She'd let sexual attraction and desire run amok. And letting her brain take the back seat had knocked her off balance.

She'd spent years proving that she was a born

leader who could accomplish anything a man could do—and she'd often done it better. But she'd just taken a giant step backward when it came to proving anything.

To make matters worse, not only was Steven an amazing lover, the best she'd ever had, he'd also become a kind and supportive friend, one who'd gone so far as to offer to marry her, just so she could save face.

But friends didn't sleep together. Nor did they stir up the yearnings and romantic feelings Ellie had begun to have. And that left her uneasy and a little disoriented.

The bathroom walls began to close in on her, and all she wanted to do was escape to a quiet place where she could think herself out of the corner she'd just backed into. But where could she go? Reporters and bloggers were just waiting to pounce on her, so she would probably end up driving around town until she came up with a better game plan.

After running a brush through her hair and applying some lip gloss, she slipped into a pale green T-shirt and a pair of black yoga pants, her baby belly stretching the waistband to the limit. She opened the bathroom door and stepped into the hall, only to find Steven standing there, shirtless and wearing a pair of jeans, the top button undone. She stopped dead in her tracks, like a possum facing an oncoming car in the street, heart pounding and having nowhere to run.

Guilt and insecurity—feelings she rarely, if ever, experienced—slammed into her.

"Ellie," he said, his voice soft yet husky. "What's wrong?"

Nothing.

Everything.

It's hard to put it into words.

"We need to talk," he said.

He was probably right, but not now. Not until she'd had some time to think. And not until he put on a shirt and covered that broad chest and those taut abs.

She looked everywhere but at him. "There's not much to say. I shouldn't have let that happen. I wasn't thinking clearly." She still wasn't. Making love with Steven had jumbled every thought in her head.

What's worse, it had messed with her heart, too.

He folded his arms across his bare chest, not nearly hiding it from view, and shifted his weight to one hip. "Didn't you enjoy what we just did?"

Her cheeks warmed, and she winced. He had to have heard her moaning softly, had to have realized she'd connected deeply with him as he'd climaxed along with her. If she told him she hadn't taken any pleasure in their lovemaking, he'd know she was lying.

"I enjoyed it as much as you did, but that's not the point." She combed her fingers through her hair, snagging a nail on a tangle she'd failed to brush out. Why hadn't she taken the time to pull it into a neat, tidy bun? Her brain worked better when she dressed professionally, and her words came much easier.

But she'd be darned if she could sound the least bit coherent while the man she'd just made love with stood half-naked in front of her. But she may as well spit it out. "Making love, as good as it was, only makes things worse. This is supposed to be a fake engagement, Steven. We had an agreement, and what we just did makes it feel more real."

"We're both consenting adults. What's wrong with acting on the attraction that's been brewing between us?"

He had a point, but she was about to make another romantic mistake, this one worse than the one she'd made with Mike, because it could lead to heartbreak—*hers* and obviously not his.

Steven opened his arms, clearly expecting her to walk into his embrace, to lay her head on his shoulder, but she couldn't seem to move. The Rambling Rose mayor insisted that she stand firm, while the child who lived within, the frightened little girl who'd once had to fend for herself in a run-down apartment, urged her to go to him, to accept the comfort he offered.

But Ellie no longer needed anyone to rescue her. Nor did she let people take care of her, like Steven had been doing the past couple of weeks. His compassion appeased the inner child, but it flustered the hell out of the city leader.

Steven wasn't giving up, nor did he lower his arms, but their face-off didn't last long. For some damned reason, she couldn't resist him. She eased forward and stepped into his embrace, accepting his comfort, just as she'd done when he'd offered his hospitality and friendship.

As she breathed in his woodsy scent, as his strong, warm arms enveloped her, she couldn't seem to absorb the peace and security she needed, and the whole fake marriage idea seemed more ludicrous than ever.

How could she only pretend to be in love with Steven when she was falling in love with him for real? And to make matters worse, she felt awful about misleading people, deceiving them.

Especially him.

Steven held her close and caressed her back. When he whispered, his warm breath stirred her hair. "Feeling better now?"

"A little." But not nearly enough.

He pressed a kiss against her temple, which helped a wee bit more. "Then I'll hold you until you're back on track and ready to tackle the world again."

Would she ever be back to normal? There was a big struggle going on in her brain. Love versus friendship. Right versus wrong. Truth versus lies.

She knew what she needed to do. Her parents had taught her well.

It's always best to tell the truth. It's easier to keep your story straight.

Papa's words echoed in her head, spurring her on, telling her exactly how to proceed.

"This whole marriage thing has gotten way out of hand," she said.

"The wedding is on Sunday, Ellie. It's too late to backpedal now. But I don't think that's the only thing troubling you."

He was right. But did she dare admit that she no longer knew the woman she'd become? That she was uneasy about being pregnant with another man's baby, caught up in a marriage of convenience and falling for a fake fiancé who thought sex was only meant for fun?

But their ruse had gathered too much steam already. The flowers and cake had been ordered. Steven's family from Florida was flying into San Antonio on Saturday evening. Mama had bought the perfect dress.

And so had Daria, who should be saving her money rather than spending it. Even Papa had gotten on board sooner than anyone had expected him to and had asked a guy he knew to play the guitar during the ceremony.

No, Steven was right. It was too late to do anything about it now. Not unless she wanted to turn a big mistake into one hot mess.

Chapter Twelve

Last night, at a quiet dinner party in the main part of the house, Steven had introduced Ellie to his parents, brother and sisters who'd traveled from Florida to attend the wedding. Ellie had been a little nervous about meeting them, but she shouldn't have been. They'd been nothing but kind, friendly and accepting.

David Fortune, who'd made millions in the video game industry, had silver-streaked hair and wore wire-rimmed glasses. The tall, well-dressed man appeared to be a little nerdy, but he was friendly and seemed genuinely happy about the wedding.

His wife, Marci, was an attractive woman in her mid-fifties. She seemed a bit shy and reserved, but greeted Ellie with a warm smile. "It's nice to meet you. I wish David and I could stay longer than a couple of days. But we'll be back to visit in the upcoming months. We're looking forward to getting to know you."

Wiley, Steven's younger brother who'd also been adopted by David, had arrived on the same flight. The triplets, however, were moving to Rambling Rose, so they'd rented a trailer and driven out. With the restaurant opening in May, the three sisters were eager to get settled so they could oversee the construction of Provisions, the trendy new eatery, and make sure it was built to their specifications. At twenty-three years old, they were pretty young to be taking on such a big project, but they seemed to know what they were doing.

The triplets were also identical, with straight blonde hair, blue eyes and nicely curving figures. Their parents and siblings had no problem telling them apart, but Ellie doubted if she'd ever be able to do so. Even though they'd had on different outfits last night, she'd still had trouble remembering who was wearing what.

"Megan, Nicole and I would like to hang with you guys this evening," Ashley had said about twenty minutes after their arrival, "but we need to unpack. We have a lot to do in the morning."

They would be busy, all right. Steven had asked them to whip up an after-wedding meal, and they'd jumped at the chance to show off their cooking skills.

It hadn't taken long for Ellie to decide that she liked Steven's family, and the evening had gone well. They'd wholeheartedly welcomed her into the fold, wishing her and Steven a lifetime of happiness, which left her feeling awkward and guilty. How would they feel when they learned the marriage wouldn't last?

Still, the sun came up on Sunday morning, and the wedding plans began to take shape.

At three o'clock, Ellie stood at the open sliding door and scanned the lawn, where the wedding guests sat in white rental chairs, facing the gazebo that had been adorned with greenery and yellow roses.

Papa stood on the patio, waiting to walk her down the grassy aisle, his brown eyes glistening as if holding back tears. "You make a beautiful bride, *mija*," he told her when she made her way out to him. "I always knew you would."

"Thank you, Papa." She kissed his cheek. "You look so handsome in that new suit. You're the perfect father of the bride."

"I wasn't so perfect at first. I'm sorry I wasn't more supportive."

"That's okay. I should have come to you and Mama months ago. I'm sorry, too."

"That's all behind us, *mija*." He nodded toward the gazebo, where the ceremony would take place. "Wiley walked your mother down the aisle and escorted her to our seats in the front row. And Daria's taken her place up front, although I can't believe you let her bring that dog, let alone walk him down the aisle on a leash."

Ellie smiled. "Don't you think Tank looks cute with that yellow Western bandanna tied around his neck?"

Papa clucked his tongue, but not in a disapproving way. "At least he matches the wedding party."

"He should," Ellie said. "He's a part of it."

Papa offered his arm. "Are you ready to do this?"

No. She wasn't at all ready. She wanted to bolt, to run for the hills and escape. But when she looked at the man who'd rescued her from foster care and provided her with affection, a happy home and everything a child could ever need, tears filled her eyes. "I love you, Papa. I don't know how to thank you for all you and Mama have done for me."

He pressed a kiss on her brow. "You've already thanked us by growing up to be a beautiful young woman with a heart for your family and for the community."

As they started across the yard to the grassy aisle, Ellie looked at the gazebo. The yellow roses that adorned it were pretty, but she'd chosen the color that represented friendship. At least there was one wedding prop that reflected truth and reality.

She glanced at the yellow rosebuds in her bouquet, another reminder of the bittersweet situation she'd agreed to, the fake union she was about to take part in.

Her heart stalled for a moment, then it began to rumble, sending a rush of adrenaline coursing through her veins.

She ought to stop the madness here and now. Yet she pressed her lips together and clutched Papa's arm as if it might be the only thing keeping her on the straight and narrow.

As they took the short walk from the house to the grassy aisle, the guitarist began to strum an instrumental melody. Mama stood, and the wedding guests got to their feet, too. Ellie did her best to smile, while she focused on the gazebo, where Pastor Ecklund, a short, gray-haired man with a ruddy complexion, stood front and center, facing her with a happy smile.

Daria, who'd chosen a floral-print sundress with a yellow background, stood to the minister's right, with Tank sitting at her feet, the Western bandanna giving the black pup a splash of color.

Steven and his father stood on the minister's left. David Fortune looked classy in his dark suit and yellow boutonniere. But it was Steven, who'd never looked more handsome in his black Western jacket and slacks, white shirt, and bolo tie, who drew her full attention. When an appreciative smile crossed his face, a bevy of butterflies took flight in her tummy.

What were they doing? Was there any way to stop the madness before it was too late?

"Who gives this woman away?" Pastor Ecklund asked.

"Her mother and I," Papa said as he handed her off to Steven.

The two of them turned to face the minister. They'd asked him to keep things short and sweet. And he did just that. In a matter of minutes, they'd made the vows they'd never keep—to love each other, for better, for worse, for richer, for poorer, in sickness and in health…as long as they both should live.

Tears sprung to Ellie's eyes. People would think they were tears of joy, rather than sorrow. Because she actually meant the vows she spoke.

"If anyone here has a reason why these two shouldn't be married," Pastor Ecklund said, "speak now or forever hold your peace."

Ellie had a reason. A big one. This wasn't a marriage based on love. It was based on a lie, and it would end in divorce. Should she speak now? This was her chance—the last one she'd have.

Her lips parted to object, but when she looked at Steven, when she saw the radiant smile on his face and the sparkle that lit up his blue eyes, the words wouldn't form.

"I now pronounce you man and wife," Pastor Ecklund said.

Like any loving, eager groom, Steven took her in his arms and blessed her lips with a sweet, husbandly kiss, ending the ceremony.

As far as anyone knew, the wedding had turned out to be everything a bride could hope for.

Too bad it had all been a sham.

After the ceremony, the bride and groom greeted their guests together, thanking them for their support and good wishes. Then they split up to mingle separately.

There'd been times when Steven had wished that he hadn't proposed to Ellie as a way to help her avoid a sticky political situation. But that wasn't because he had any regrets himself. Ellie, however, seemed to be plagued with them, and he hated to see her so uneasy. He'd thought making love the other night would have made her feel better, but she claimed it had made things worse.

He supposed that's why he felt compelled to stick so close to her during the reception. Even now, as he stood off to the side with his brothers and dad, he was so damned focused on the bride that he was having a difficult time following the conversation.

His father made a comment, and his brothers laughed. Steven managed to smile and nod as if he'd actually heard him speak and caught the joke.

As a man who'd always tried hard to earn the name he shared with Callum and Dillon, he usually listened intently and carried his own weight in a family conversation. But he couldn't seem to do that today.

He scanned the yard again and spotted Ellie talking to Daria, that goofy little pup tethered to a yellow leash and sniffing at the grass. Both the women wore smiles, so he assumed Ellie was holding up okay.

"Steven," his father said, finally drawing his full attention. "You did well."

At what? Was he talking about business? If he questioned his dad, everyone would know he'd been lost in thought. And he wasn't about to explain why.

"Ellie isn't just bright," his father added, "she's beautiful, too. You picked a good one. I hope you'll both be as happy as your mother and I are."

"Thanks," Steven said, his gaze returning to

his bride, who was a vision in her white dress, one she'd chosen because it only revealed a hint of her baby bump.

"I'm a little surprised that you didn't buy her an engagement ring," his dad said. "You found time to pull of a beautiful wedding in record time. You even went so far as to buy a plain gold band."

"Ellie wanted something simple."

His father's head tilted, and his brow creased. "She doesn't seem like a keep-it-simple gal to me."

She wasn't. She was beautifully complex, and she deserved an engagement ring, even if the marriage didn't last. "I'm going to surprise her with a diamond at Christmas," he said.

Would they still be married then? He'd once thought so, but after the past few days, he wasn't so sure. She might be smiling and wearing white, but she was still on edge, still uneasy. That's why he hadn't let her out of his sight.

He'd actually suggested they go on a honeymoon, which would have given them a good reason to cut out early, but Ellie said that was out of the question. She'd been away from city hall for too long as it was. In fact, she planned to return to the office tomorrow morning. Hopefully, she was ready to face the press.

Neither of them mentioned the wedding night, but Steven looked forward to having one. They hadn't made love since the first time, but he couldn't see why she'd object.

Either way, he'd like to take her away from the crowd. But that would have to wait. Ashley, Megan and Nicole were in the main kitchen, putting the finishing touches on the post-wedding meal, which was yet to come, along with the cake.

"If you'll excuse me," Steven told his father and brothers, "I'm going to get something to drink. It's been a long day."

As he strode toward the portable bar the rental company had set up, he scanned the yard again.

Ellie and Daria still stood off to the side, away from most of the wedding guests and talking quietly. He liked Daria, and she'd proven to be a good friend to Ellie, the perfect maid of honor, it seemed.

Manny, the family cook and caretaker, approached the bar and stood beside Steven. "Nice wedding."

"Thanks."

"What can I get you?" the attractive blond bartender asked.

"I'll have a glass of red wine," Manny said.

The bartender reached for a bottle of the Mendoza Winery merlot. "And what'll you have, Mr. Fortune?"

"A cold beer."

While he waited, Steven glanced over his shoulder and saw his sister Stephanie approach Ellie and Daria. Funny, but instead of returning to his dad and his brothers, he'd much rather join that conversation.

As Ellie and Daria chatted, Stephanie Fortune approached them. The pretty blonde seemed to glow with excitement over her engagement to Acton Donovan. From what Ellie had heard, she and Acton had recently announced that they'd be having a baby soon.

Stephanie zeroed in on Tank. "Would you look at that sweet puppy. He looks so cute wearing that yellow bandanna." She stooped to give the rascally pup a scratch behind the ears. "How're you doing, buddy? I'm so glad you found a good home."

"He certainly did," Ellie told her new sister-in-law. "He's a little spoiled and can be a rascal at times, but he's sweet and lovable. He's also doubled in size since Daria adopted him."

Stephanie straightened just as Becky approached them with a grin. "What's going on over here?"

Ellie had come to like Callum's wife and tossed her a smile. "Not much. Just a little girl talk. Please join us."

"It was a lovely wedding," Becky said. "And you rock that wedding dress."

"Thank you." Ellie's hand lifted to her belly, but she caught herself before drawing any attention to her baby bump.

Becky turned to Stephanie. "How're you hold-ing up? I know it hasn't been easy."

A wisp of sadness crossed the vet assistant's face. "Okay, I guess. I miss baby Linus."

"Baby Linus?" Ellie asked.

"He's the baby Stephanie fostered," Becky said. "During the grand opening of the pediatric center, a woman named Laurel went into premature labor. She was stabilized, and Dr. Green sent her to the hospital in San Antonio to deliver, because they have a NICU. Then, not even a month later, Laurel left Linus on the doorstep of the pediatric center with a note that mentioned keeping her child safe and something about finding his rightful home at Fortune's Foundling Hospital."

Ellie furrowed her brow. "But the foundling home isn't there anymore. You'd think everyone would know that. In fact, Steven purchased an old scrapbook at Mariana's Market that has a newspa-per article in it about the hospital and its closing."

"Apparently Laurel wasn't thinking clearly," Becky said.

Stephanie rubbed her tummy, much the way Ellie found herself doing these days and, in a wist-ful voice, said, "I loved that baby."

"I know you did." Becky placed a gentle hand on Stephanie's shoulder. "I'm so sorry you had to let him go."

Stephanie's eyes filled with tears. "It's weird,

though. Laurel had implied that Eric, the father, wouldn't be pleased about the baby, but he was actually thrilled. I wasn't prepared for that. And it broke my heart to let him go."

"You'll never forget that sweet baby," Becky said, "but at least you and Acton will have one of your own soon."

Stephanie sniffled, blinked back her tears and offered a wistful smile. "That's true."

"Whatever happened to Laurel?" Ellie asked.

Stephanie shrugged. "We may never know. The authorities haven't been able to find her. And I hate to say it, but I don't have a good feeling about her disappearance."

Ellie cringed at the thought of a baby being abandoned and of something happening to the young mother, even if things seemed to have turned out okay in the long run.

"How's Linus doing?" Becky asked. "Have you talked to Eric?"

"Yes, I have. And to be honest, I'm a little worried."

"Why?" Becky asked.

"Eric thinks Linus isn't growing fast enough."

"That could be due to his prematurity," Becky said.

Stephanie sighed. "Maybe so. I sure hope that's all it is."

So did Ellie. Compared to what Baby Linus had been through, and whatever his birth mother had

gone through or might still be going through Ellie's worries about her own situation paled. And it
seemed to put things back into perspective. Ellie
had her health. She also had a loving family and
loyal friends. And she would soon have a baby to
hold and to love. She and Steven may have entered
a fake marriage, but Baby George was real.

For the first time since learning she was pregnant, she decided not to worry about what people
might think or what the press might print. Nor did
she care if the community learned that she'd entered a fake marriage with a man who only wanted
to be friends.

She stole a glance across the lawn and spotted
Steven near the bar, holding a long-neck bottle
of beer. As he talked to the bartender, an attractive blonde in her late twenties or early thirties he
laughed at something she said, and a twinge of
jealousy gripped Ellie.

On the outside, he might look like a happy
groom. But he was rich, handsome and still single at heart.

She should be thankful for his friendship, as
well as his efforts to help her face her parents and
the community. And she was. But she'd fallen head
over heart for a man who didn't love her. Not the
way a real husband should.

This was supposed to be a happy day, and dammit, Ellie would force herself to look on the bright side—and there was one.

After all, she told herself, *it's not about me. Nor is it about Steven.*

Right now, the only thing that mattered was the very real little boy she'd be bringing into the world in four and a half months. And she could certainly be happy about that.

Chapter Thirteen

For a fake wedding that had been pulled together in record time, the ceremony, as well as the entire afternoon and evening, had turned out a lot nicer than Ellie had expected it to. And even more surprising, the Fortunes not only had welcomed her into the fold, they'd accepted her parents as well.

The two families, one ultra wealthy from Fort Lauderdale and the other blue collar from Rambling Rose, had very little in common, yet they seemed to hit it off.

If they hadn't, and the laughter and friendly conversations had only been for show, then they were better actors than the bride and groom.

The triplets had put on an amazing wedding dinner that included lobster and filet mignon. Nicole, the self-taught sous chef, was every bit as talented as Steven had said she was. And Ellie had no doubt that Provisions, their restaurant, would be popular and jam-packed once it opened in May.

In fact, the wedding had gone so well that Ellie could almost believe their marriage would last. That was, if Steven were to fall in love with her. If he didn't, then the divorce they'd planned to get in the future was the only option.

By the time the evening festivities wrapped up, Ellie had been ready to retreat to the guest room and call it a day. But before she could start down the hall, Steven had tossed her a dazzling, sexy smile, and her energy level rose.

"Your bed or mine?" he'd asked.

She hesitated, but only for a moment. "Yours."

He took her hand and led her to his room, where he stopped near the bed. He cupped her face with both hands and kissed her softly. Then he reached up and unpinned her once elegant twist, letting her hair tumble down, over her shoulders.

She turned her back to him and, using her right hand, she swept the loose tresses to one side, giving him access to the buttons. "I'm going to need some help."

"That would be a pleasure." He slowly and deliberately undid each tiny pearl button. When the fabric gapped, he pressed a kiss on her shoulder, his breath warm against her skin. Then he helped her remove the gown.

Wearing only a pair of white lace panties and a matching bra, she turned to face him again. Their eyes fixed on each other as they removed the last of their clothing, one piece at a time.

When they were both naked, Ellie couldn't help scanning her husband's handsome face, his broad shoulders and taut abs. Steven Fortune was a hottie on any given day of the week. But standing naked, just steps from his bed, he was an arousing sight to behold.

When he opened his arms, she stepped into his embrace—skin to skin, her breasts pressed against his chest.

He kissed her deeply, thoroughly, as if this was a real wedding night, as if she was his real bride and he was her groom. His tongue swept into her mouth, meeting her own, twisting, dipping, tasting with a hunger that couldn't be sated with a kiss.

As if sensing her need, her desire, Steven lifted her in his arms and laid her on top of his bed. He joined her, and they took up where they'd left off— tongues mating, breaths mingling, hearts racing, hands seeking and caressing.

A thrill of excitement shivered through her, and an empty ache settled deep in her core.

"I want you," she said. She needed him, too.

And even though the events leading up to today had been based on a lie, her words were true, her hunger undeniable.

As he hovered over her, ready to give her what she asked for, yet not all that she wanted, she opened for him. He entered her, filling her, pleasing her with each thrust, each stroke.

Yet at the same time, she held back, afraid to put her heart and soul into their lovemaking.

How could she give him her all, when their wedding night wasn't real, and their marriage wouldn't last?

He drove into her, and she arched up, again and again until they both reached a peak. She let go, and they came together in a glorious, star-bursting climax that nearly knocked the earth off its axis.

Ellie didn't dare speak, didn't dare move, as they lay amid tangled sheets, the scent of their lovemaking in each breath they took. Even as her world seemed to right itself, she lay cradled in his arms, her head resting on his chest, his hand on her hip.

Making love had been good, but the something she'd held back had been missing.

If Steven sensed anything was off, he didn't say. He might have assumed that she was exhausted from a long, stressful week. And that was certainly true because she fell asleep and didn't wake up until morning.

Ellie hadn't set an alarm, but she hadn't needed to. The sunlight peeking through the shutter slats woke her at eight. After a stretch and a yawn, she climbed out of bed and padded to the bathroom, where she showered and got ready for the day. She dressed in her favorite business suit, although this was the last day she'd be wearing it for a while. Her belly felt as if it had doubled in size in the last week.

She wasn't sure when Steven left. He'd said he had an early meeting at the Paz job site. Dillon was concerned the building might not pass the electrical inspection, so they'd called in the foreman and one of the contractors to discuss the problem.

Before leaving the privacy and comfort of Steven's living quarters, she fixed a healthy breakfast of yogurt, granola and fruit. Then she headed to the foyer to let herself out.

"Ellie?" Steven's mother called out from the main part of the house. "Is that you?"

Her steps slowed just short of the front door. "Yes, Marci. It's me."

The sweet, middle-aged woman approached with a coffee cup in hand. "I was hoping I'd get to see you before you left for work."

Ellie's radar went on high alert. Things had been almost too perfect over the last twenty-four hours, so she waited for the other shoe to drop.

"Is something wrong?" she asked.

"No, not at all. I just wanted to let you know how nice it is to see my son so happy. And so much in love."

Marci reached out, took Ellie's hand in hers and gave it a gentle squeeze. A warm smile brightened her face. "We wouldn't have missed your special day for the world, honey. I'm just sorry we have to return to Florida this afternoon. I'd love to get to know you better. But don't worry. I'm sure we'll be back soon. I can't wait to get to know the twins better. Aren't they precious?"

"They sure are."

"And I suspect Stephanie and Acton will be getting married soon." Marci burst into a rosy-cheeked, bright-eyed smile. "Can you believe it? They'll be having a baby, too. I can't wait to go home to my friends and boast about my grand-children."

Accepting Stephanie's child was a given. But would Marci accept Ellie's son as easily and un-conditionally as she had Becky's daughters? That was, if her marriage to Steven lasted more than a few months.

Ellie liked to think that Marci would. Taking care not to bump the cup in the older woman's hand, she gave Steven's mother a hug and thanked her again. "Have a safe flight home, Marci."

"Thank you, honey. Have a good day."

Ellie let herself out of the house and headed

to her car. Twenty minutes later, she arrived at city hall and parked in her reserved space. She'd no more than entered the building when a short, heavyset reporter rushed to her.

"Mayor Hernandez," the reporter asked, "rumor has it you and Steven Fortune got married over the weekend. Any truth to that?"

Ellie answered without slowing her pace. "Yes, that's true. We had a small wedding yesterday. Just family and a few close friends were there."

Undaunted, the reporter lifted his iPhone, no doubt wanting a picture, and dogged her through the spacious lobby. "Is it true that you're expecting a baby? And that you're already five months along?"

The question struck a low blow, and while Ellie wanted to breeze right past the guy and enter the privacy of her office, the time had come to face facts and the community at large.

She stopped abruptly, turned and faced him, just as the camera flashed. "Steven and I are looking forward to the birth of our son in mid-August."

The camera flashed again, but she ignored it and strode to the reception desk, where Iris sat, taking in the scene. "Do I have any messages?"

"Yes, three of them." The receptionist reached for several pink slips that sat next to the While You Were Out pad. "Gosh, Ellie—I mean, Mayor Hernandez—I had no idea you were dating Mr.

Fortune until just recently. Things sure happened fast between you. I'm surprised you were able to keep your relationship a secret."

Ellie stiffened. "My personal life is none of your business, Iris. And if you'd like to keep your job, you'd better remember that."

The nosy receptionist let out a little gasp. "I'm sorry. I didn't mean to overstep."

Yeah. Right. Ellie snatched her messages and continued to her office. Unfortunately, Iris wasn't the only one who'd be making assumptions and doing the math. But it was too damned late to worry about that now.

As the days passed, there'd been mixed reactions to Ellie's announcement about her marriage and the upcoming birth of her son. Her Q ratings had never been higher. And from what she'd heard, most of her constituents considered her and Steven to be local celebrities and an attractive couple. Those were the friends, colleagues and townspeople who embraced the news and considered the wedding and the upcoming birth of her son to be blessed events. But there was still a vocal minority who believed that she'd sold out.

At times, Ellie had to agree with them. Not that she'd compromised her principles when it came to her position as the Rambling Rose mayor. In that respect, she never wavered and continued to look out for the city's best interests. But when it came to her personal life, it was a completely different story.

Against her better judgment, she'd married a man who didn't love her, a decision that betrayed every marital value she espoused.

On the outside, things seemed to be working out okay. She and Steven were more than compatible in bed. On top of that, he was kind, considerate and fun to talk to. She had to admit he was the best fake husband ever, and with each passing day, she grew to love him more. But he hadn't given her any reason to believe that his feelings for her had changed at all, and Ellie couldn't continue in a relationship like that. It was time to confront him and ask how long he intended to keep up the charade, the pretext. Did he expect them to remain friends and lovers indefinitely? Or had something changed between them?

If he couldn't give her the right answers, the ones she hoped to hear, then she would just have to make it easy on them both.

That morning, while Steven brewed a pot of coffee before leaving for one of the job sites, Ellie appeared in the small kitchen. "I'm glad you haven't left yet."

"Hey, you're up early." He turned and blessed her with a bright-eyed grin. "It's only five o'clock, and the sun isn't even up yet."

"I need to talk to you, and I didn't want to wait until this evening."

"All right. What do you want to talk about?"

"About us. Our marriage." They'd spent nights making love and falling asleep in each other's arms. Surely she wasn't the only one who felt it, who cherished it.

"There's not much to talk about," he said, as he removed a disposable heat-resistant cup from the pantry and filled it with coffee. "I'm happy."

She folded her arms across her chest. "What does that mean?"

He placed the lid on top of his to-go cup and snapped it in place. "It means I like having you here. I'm comfortable with the situation and I'm not in a hurry to do anything differently."

"You're *comfortable*?" she asked.

He set the cup back on the counter and turned to face her. "You're not?"

Ellie didn't like words that translated to mediocre, words like *nice* and *comfortable*. She'd always been an overachiever and never settled for just so-so.

"No," she said, "I'm having a problem with it."

"Wow. I didn't see that coming. You aren't happy?"

"It's not that. It's just that I don't like facing an uncertain future. I need to know what to expect and how to plan for it. And I don't have any idea how long this relationship will last."

"You're thinking too hard," he said.

"That's what I do, Steven. I think. I plan. I make lists and follow them to a T. I don't like open-ended solutions."

"If you're worried that I'll back out on our agreement, don't be. I have no intention of breaking it." He reached for her hand, lifted it to his lips and kissed her fingers. "I'm not going anywhere."

Maybe not yet. But how long would he stick around?

When she didn't respond, he released her hand and furrowed his brow. "Now I'm getting worried. Do you want out? Are you ready to end things?"

Not if he loved her. But the unspoken words twisted her heart into a knot, and she opted to provide him with a half-truth. "No, I'm not ready for it to end."

"Good." He swept her into his arms and gave her a quick kiss.

She kissed him back, although as far as she was concerned, it felt a little cool. A little stiff.

Apparently he hadn't noticed, because he released her, turned back to the counter and picked up his cup as if nothing had happened, as if nothing was wrong.

She'd try to do the same thing by pretending that they were back on an even keel, which wasn't easy to do when the small boat she seemed to be riding on was being tossed to and fro, making her seasick.

"What do you have planned today?" Steven asked.

"I have to go to city hall this morning, and this afternoon I have a doctor's appointment."

"Is your mother going with you again?"

"Not this time."

He seemed to think about her answer.

She felt compelled to ask if he wanted to go with her, but why would he? She wasn't his real wife. And she wasn't having *his* baby.

"I have another meeting," he said. "This one is at Provisions. So I'd better get on the road."

That must've been where his mind was just moments ago.

"I'll talk to you later," he added.

She nodded, but she wasn't so sure they had any more to talk about. He'd made his feelings clear, even if he hadn't come right out and admitted it. He liked being her friend and lover. But that was it.

And she couldn't go on this way much longer. She'd eventually blurt out her feelings and voice her regret.

Still, just as she'd done every workday since she'd moved in with him, she followed him to the foyer, where he gave her a kiss goodbye. "I'll see you tonight," he told her. "Don't worry about dinner. I'll pick up something in town and bring it home."

She nodded, although dinner was the last thing on her mind. And so was spending another night at the Fame and Fortune Ranch. Against all odds, she'd fallen in love with a man who considered their marriage a temporary arrangement.

It wasn't Steven's fault, though. They'd made a deal, and he was sticking to it. How could she be angry at him for doing everything he'd said he would do?

She was the one who'd changed the rules. But that didn't mean she had to continue playing the game.

As she walked back to their living quarters— or rather, to Steven's living quarters—she placed her hand on her belly. Did she really want to drag her baby into a situation like this?

No, she did not. And she'd be insane to continue the ruse. She had to end things with Steven, and the sooner she did so, the better. She'd always prided herself on her honesty. But what a laugh that was. She'd been deceiving everyone she'd come into contact with for months, but no one more than herself.

She returned to the bedroom and packed her things. Before dragging her suitcase, garment bags and canvas tote out to the car, she stopped at the small desk in Steven's room, opened the drawer and pulled out a pen and paper.

A personal conversation was probably in order, but she could spell out her feelings on paper much easier than she could say them to his face. So she wrote a note to explain why she was leaving. Then she left it on the kitchen table, where he would be sure to see it as soon as he got home.

Tears welled in Ellie's eyes as she drove back to town, her suitcase and bags in the trunk, her wedding dress in the back seat. As badly as she wanted to hurry home so she could vent to Daria and lick her wounds, she drove straight to her parents' house instead.

She'd been lying to the two people who loved her more than anyone else in the world. And her mom and dad deserved better from her. They'd proven their love and loyalty for years, and it was high time she trusted them enough to admit her mistakes and share her heartache.

What was wrong with her? Why had it taken her so long to figure it out? She'd never wanted to disappoint them, but she had. And worse yet, she'd disappointed herself.

As the tears streamed down her cheeks, she swiped at them with the back of her hand and continued to drive to the one place in town where everything was familiar—the white clapboard church on the corner, the elementary school she'd attended, the park where she used to play.

She turned down the tree-lined drive and continued to the three-bedroom home in which she'd grown up. Her father's old green pickup and her mother's sedan were parked in the driveway, which meant she could face them both in one fell swoop.

After parking at the curb, she took a moment to study the well-manicured lawn, the colorful flowers that lined the walkway. Then she got out of the car and headed for the front porch. Birds chirped in the treetops, announcing that winter was over and spring had come to bring new life and hope.

Ellie knocked lightly on the door, then let herself in. "Mama? Papa? It's me."

"We're in the kitchen," her mother said. "We slept in this morning, so we're having a late breakfast. Come join us."

Ellie crossed the warm, cozy living room, taking note of the mantel over the redbrick fireplace that still displayed several framed photographs of her as a child and one of her in her cap and gown at her college graduation. That was just another sign of her parents' deep love for her.

As she entered the kitchen, she found her mother frying bacon and scrambling eggs while her father sat at the table sipping coffee and reading the sports page.

"This is a nice surprise," Mama said as she

removed the frying pan from the flame. When she turned and faced Ellie, her smile faded, and a frown took its place. "You've been crying, honey. What's the matter?"

"It's a long, complicated story," Ellie said. "And I need to get it off my chest."

Her father pulled out a chair. "Have a seat, *mija*. Your mother and I have all day."

Ellie wasn't sure where to begin, but if she intended to level with her parents, she'd have to start with Mike. So she told them about the mistake she'd made in thinking he was family material, only to find out the hard way that he wasn't. She admitted that he'd fathered her baby. And then she'd shared his coldhearted response to the news.

"Was Steven angry when he found out you were pregnant with Mike's baby?" Mama asked. "Is that why you're crying?"

"He knew. And it didn't bother him."

"Then I don't understand why you're upset," Papa said. "Are you afraid the press will find out that Steven isn't the father?"

Ellie blew out a sigh. "I don't even care about that. Not anymore."

Mama poured herself a cup of coffee and took a seat at the table. "Then why are you so unhappy?"

"Steven is my friend, and he asked me to marry him so that I could save face in the community. And, like a fool, I agreed to do it, even though I knew it would end up being one more mistake in the long run."

"You married a man you didn't love?" Mama asked.

"I went into the agreement thinking of Steven as my friend, but then I fell in love with him. Unfortunately, he doesn't feel the same way about me. And I can't keep living like that, pretending that the marriage is real and that my new husband fathered my baby." An ache settled in Ellie's chest, and tears filled her eyes again.

"Pastor Ecklund is an ordained minister," Papa said. "You might not feel like the marriage is real, but like it or not, you and Steven are legally wed."

"I know, and that complicates the matter. When this stupid charade started, we agreed to get a quiet, amicable divorce after the baby was born. But under the circumstances, I think it's best if we split up now."

"And Steven's okay with that?" Mama asked.

"Why wouldn't he be? He's not the one who will have to face the press and explain to the community that he lied to them." Ellie shot a glance at Papa, then at Mama. "Worse than that, I lied to you. And I'm so sorry. I hope you'll forgive me."

"Of course we will. At least you're being truthful now." Mama reached out and patted the top of Ellie's hand. "It won't be easy being a single mom and raising a child on your own, but your father and I will stand by you every step of the way."

"Thanks, Mama. You have no idea how much I appreciate that."

"Your mother's right," Papa said. "You mean the world to us, *mija*. And so does that little boy. Just tell us how we can best support you."

Ellie blew out a sigh as another onslaught of tears began to slide down her cheeks. "I'll let you know when I figure it out. In the meantime, people are going to talk. If anyone asks why I left Steven, just tell them that it didn't work out."

For once, she'd be telling the truth. Things hadn't worked out, even though Ellie wished with all her heart that they had.

Chapter Fourteen

"What a day," Steven muttered as he drove back to the ranch. It started early and ended late, but it had been productive. The spa building had passed its final inspection, which meant the grand opening was still on track.

After leaving the office, he stopped by Peking Palace and picked up Chinese takeout. He wasn't sure what dishes Ellie liked, so he ordered a variety from the menu. They'd end up having leftovers for days, but that didn't matter.

By the time he arrived at the ranch, the sun had nearly set. Ellie's car wasn't parked in her usual spot, but he didn't think anything of it. She probably had an unexpected meeting in town. Hopefully, she'd be home soon.

Once inside the foyer, he headed to his private quarters and stopped in the kitchen. He placed both bags on the counter, then opened the fridge and pulled out a bottle of water. He unscrewed the top and took a big swig, quenching his thirst.

He considered taking a shower before he spotted a note on the table addressed to him.

> *Dear Steven,*
>
> *I'm sorry, but I can't keep living a lie. I'm not angry with you. How could I be when you've never been anything but good to me? But it's time for me to go home. I need to set up a nursery and prepare for the baby.*
>
> *I value our friendship and appreciate all you've done for me. If our marriage had been real, things might have been different. But my highest priority right now is my son. He deserves to have a loving home, and one that's permanent.*
>
> *Ellie*

The words blindsided him, and he sat down to read them again.

She'd moved out? Just like that? And without talking it over with him first, without asking him how he felt about it?

Hell, how *did* he feel about it?

Angry came to mind. Hadn't she cared enough about him or his feelings to tell him to his face? He was disappointed to find her gone. He was hurt, too, he supposed.

His head spun with other emotions he couldn't quite put his finger on. Were they still friends? Had they gone back to being at political odds?

Damn. He found the whole thing confusing. And he wasn't sure what, if anything, to do about it.

And then there was the baby. His entire family and the whole damned town thought it was his. He'd been prepared to step up to the plate, but apparently Ellie hadn't ever considered him taking an active, paternal-type role. She'd taken her mom to one of her obstetrical appointments, and even though he'd thought she might ask him to go in Alma's place this afternoon, she hadn't.

At the time, he'd been afraid to ask, afraid he might be overstepping. He'd had a busy day, but he would have shuffled things around and found the time.

She clearly preferred to go alone, and that irritated him more now than it had this morning. And it shouldn't. Hell, he wasn't the baby's father.

Yet, in some odd way, he'd begun to think that he was. How was that for losing his head over his friendship with Ellie?

He sat at the kitchen table for the longest time, the note in his hand, his brain scrambling to make sense of it all. It wasn't until his cell phone rang that the fog began to clear.

Was Ellie having second thoughts? Was she on her way home?

He glanced at the lighted display and frowned. Then he swiped his finger across the screen to accept Callum's call.

"Yeah, what is it?" he asked, anger and frustration setting a sharp edge to his tone.

"Whoa," Callum said. "I didn't mean to bother you. Is this a bad time?"

It sure as hell wasn't a good one. "What's up?"

"Nicole is cooking again tonight and asked me to find out if you and Ellie are going to join us for dinner."

"No, Ellie's...not home."

"We can always keep a couple of plates warm for you."

"Don't bother. I'll... We'll fend for ourselves."

"Is something wrong?" Callum asked. "You seemed okay when we left the office this afternoon, but something must have set you off."

"Don't worry about it." Instead of going into any more detail than that, Steven ended the call.

He hadn't meant to take out his anger on his brother. But he wasn't about to share his mixed-up thoughts with anyone. He'd rather wallow in them on his own.

And that's just what he did. He stewed over the situation all night long, tossing and turning until dawn.

The next day, at the construction trailer on the Paz job site, his brothers tiptoed around him. It hadn't taken long for the office staff and the employees to pick up on his foul mood and to steer clear of him. And that was fine with him.

Before he left for the day, Callum and Dillon finally approached him, hands on hips, their expressions serious.

"We have no idea what happened last night," Callum said, "but we can connect a few dots, especially since Ellie's car wasn't in the yard again this morning."

Steven could have explained, starting at the beginning, but it wasn't that simple. And he wasn't sure why. It might help to talk it out, but he was the oldest brother. His siblings were supposed to come to him for advice, not the other way around.

"Have you talked to Ellie?" Dillon asked.

Steven couldn't believe this. Since when was Dillon the expert on relationships? His last two hadn't gone well. Or so he'd gathered. But Steven bit back a snappy retort. He might be angry and all kinds of mixed up, but he wasn't so off balance that he'd intentionally hurt his younger brother.

So he shook it off the best he could. "There's nothing to talk about, guys. Ellie and I just need some time apart."

Then he walked out the door and strode toward his pickup. It wasn't supposed to end this way. Nor was it supposed to hurt. For a fake marriage, the breakup felt pretty damned real.

It had been two long days since Ellie had left the ranch, and Steven still didn't feel any better about her leaving, about that damned note she wrote, about the way his queen-size bed had grown bigger and colder without her in it.

Even when he'd holed up at Fortune Brothers Construction and tried to keep his mind on work, he felt her absence. And that didn't make any sense.

A knock sounded at the door of the modular, drawing him from his thoughts. He would have let someone else answer, but everyone else had taken off early, no doubt chased off by his crappy mood.

"What is it?" he asked.

"It's Alma Hernandez."

Steven's heart jumped to his throat then dropped to his gut. Had something happened to Ellie or the baby?

He rolled back his desk chair, got to his feet and crossed the room in three steps. He swung open the door and found Alma standing there, holding her purse in both hands.

"I don't want to keep you from your work," she said, "so I'll make this quick."

"No problem. Please, come in." He stepped aside, and when she entered, he closed the door to give them privacy.

He strode to the chair that sat across the desk and moved a stack of files and a folded blueprint he'd piled on it.

"I'm sorry for the mess. I don't usually get visitors here. Please. Have a seat."

As the retired schoolteacher complied, he wheeled his chair around the desk and sat next to her. "What's going on? Is Ellie okay?"

"She's not sick, if that's what you mean. But she's not the least bit okay. She's concerned about the divorce."

Divorce. The harsh sound of the word slammed into him. They'd talked about separating down the road, and of course, they'd planned to do it legally and file the necessary paperwork with the court. But in Steven's mind, "down the road" hadn't meant a week after the wedding.

"What's she worried about? I won't fight her, if that's what she's afraid of. I just wish she would have talked to me. We might have…" He sucked in a deep breath, then blew it out. "We made a deal, and I'm willing to follow through on it."

"Is that what you want?" Alma asked. "To follow through on the agreement?"

"I don't understand why you're asking me that question," he said. "Ellie's the one who left, and I'll admit I wasn't happy about it. If she had something on her mind, she should've talked to me in person. Instead, she left a Dear John letter that didn't shed much light on her thoughts and feelings."

Alma studied him as if he were one of her students, as if he'd stayed on the playground after recess was over and the rest of the kids had returned to class. She seemed to be considering the proper punishment, only that wasn't necessary. Ellie had already given him the ultimate time-out.

"Do you care for my daughter?" Alma asked.

"Yes, of course I do. I wouldn't have married her if I didn't."

"Do you *love* her?"

The word crept into his chest and shimmied up and down his spine. He had feelings for Ellie. Deep ones. And it had hurt like the devil when she left.

"I might. I'm not sure. I..." Steven raked a hand through his hair. He sure as hell felt something for her.

"At the wedding," Alma said, "I saw you watch Ellie as she walked down the aisle. The expression on your face didn't seem fake. And neither did your smile or the happiness glimmering in your eyes. Unless you're bound for the Broadway stage, I suspect you're feeling more than friendship for her."

She was right. His feelings ran deeper than that. "I'm not supposed to feel more than friendship. That was the deal."

"If you love her—or if you think it might come to that one day—I suggest you fight for her."

Fight who? Steven's hand fisted, and his brow furrowed. "Did that bastard come back from South America?"

"No, and I don't expect he ever will. The battle I was referring to is the one going on inside you."

He was definitely struggling. And it sounded like Ellie was, too. But a man had pride. And she was the one who'd thrown in the towel.

"What's holding you back?" Alma asked.

Steven merely sat there, pondering her words, as well as his thoughts and feelings.

"Is it the baby? I know it isn't yours."

"No, that's not it. That poor little guy can't help it if his biological dad is an ass."

"That's true. But a lot of men wouldn't want to take on someone else's responsibility."

David Fortune had. He'd adopted both Steven and Wiley, and he'd treated them both like his biological sons. Steven had appreciated being a Fortune and had wanted to prove himself worthy of the name.

But in reality, what had he been trying to prove?

David had treated all the boys the same. He went to parent-teacher conferences, watched baseball games, sent them all to camp, paid for private lessons, listened to problems. And he'd never once complained.

Steven blew out a sigh.

"My daughter has a stubborn streak," Alma said. "And I can see that you do, too. She's in love with you, but I'm not sure if she'll be the first to admit it. And I'm fairly certain that you feel the same way about her. Don't let your pride get in the way of your happiness." Alma wheeled her chair back and stood. "I hope you'll forgive me for showing up uninvited. I'm usually not one to meddle, but I couldn't help myself this time. I'll go now—and leave you to think about what I said. But no matter what you decide or how this ends, my husband and I have the greatest respect for you. We think you're a good man, an honorable one."

"Thanks." He wasn't sure if he was thanking her for the compliment she left him with or for coming to talk to him. But he stood and walked her to the door.

Before she could exit, Steven stopped her. "If Ellie loves me, then why did she leave?"

Alma smiled softly. "You'll need to ask her that." Then she turned and walked away, leaving him stunned and with a lot to think about.

* * *

Ellie had gone to visit her parents again this afternoon, but her mom was just leaving to run an errand. Ellie told them she'd come back another day, but Papa insisted they focus on something else for a change.

"It'll be good for you to get out," he'd said.

When she agreed, he'd taken her window-shopping for baby furniture. Then he'd driven her to the hardware store to pick up some paint samples to take with them.

He'd been right. Spending the day with him had helped a lot. She still felt incredibly sad when she thought about Steven and what might have been, but her father had helped her to realize she had a lot to be thankful for, a lot to look forward to.

On the way home, Ellie called Daria to ask if she had given dinner any thought.

"Hey," Daria said. "I'm glad you called. I've got some news. And it's about to bubble right out of me. The CEO of the car wash chain that purchased Happy Suds just called me and asked if I'd like to work for them."

"That's great news. But I thought they already had an accountant."

"They do, but his wife is an officer in the army, and she just received orders to spend the next three years in Germany. So he and the entire family are going with her. He's leaving in three weeks, so the

CEO wants me to come to Houston now so I can work with him before he goes. That way, we can make a smooth transition."

"When are you leaving?"

"Actually, I'm already packed. The company is going to put me up in an apartment in Houston for the next couple of months. Then, once I get the lay of the land, I'll be able to buy a place of my own. Only thing is, I'll have to travel some. But I'm okay with that."

"You sound excited."

"I am. The pay is good. And they plan to buy more car washes, so there's a chance for upward mobility."

"I'm happy for you," Ellie said. "But I'll miss you."

"Houston isn't that far away. I can visit sometimes. And you can stay with me, too. But I have a favor to ask."

"What's that?"

"I can't take Tank with me."

Ellie couldn't tell her no. Besides, she liked the little rascal. "I might have to ask my parents to puppy-sit when I'm at work, but they probably won't mind."

"That would be great," Daria said. "I have a hair appointment in about ten minutes, so I need to run. Then I'm headed out of town. Can we talk more about this tomorrow?"

"Sure. I'm not going anywhere."

Five minutes later, Ellie arrived home and let herself into the house. Daria had already left, but Tank greeted her at the door, tail wagging.

She stooped to give him a scratch behind the ear. "Looks like it's just you and me, Tank. And the baby makes three."

Tank cocked his head to the side, clearly not understanding.

"Come on," Ellie told him. "I'll let you outside so you can go pee."

She'd just opened the slider to let the puppy into the backyard when the doorbell rang. It was probably the neighbor kids wanting to play with Tank. So she crossed the small living room, her bare feet padding on the hardwood floor, and opened the door.

Instead of the two red-haired children she'd expected to see, she spotted Steven standing on the stoop, his Stetson in hand. Her heart dropped to her feet, and she feared her lower jaw did the same dang thing.

"Can I come in?" he asked.

She stepped aside, her heart pounding to the beat of a rock band, and allowed him to enter.

"I've missed you," he said.

She'd missed him, too. But that didn't mean she'd move back to the Fame and Fortune Ranch.

She swept her hand toward the living room. "Come in and sit down."

He strode to the sofa, placed his hat on the coffee table and took a seat. She kept her distance. She'd be able to keep a clearer mind when she wasn't breathing in his musky scent, when he wasn't close enough to touch.

"How are you doing?" he asked.

"Fine. I saw the doctor yesterday, and he said everything's good—the baby's growing and healthy."

"I'm glad to hear that, but I was actually talking about your feelings."

His bluntness took her aback, and she realized he was talking about the goodbye letter she'd left him. It had seemed like the right thing to do at the time, but she suspected cowardice had played a large part in it.

Unwilling to show any vulnerability, any guilt, she shrugged a single shoulder. "I'm hanging in there. I had a nice talk with my parents the other day. And I spent yesterday afternoon with my dad. So I'm moving along."

"How are you feeling about me?" he asked. "About us."

She'd be darned if she'd blurt out how she really felt. That she missed him terribly. That her heart ached for him. Her body, too.

"You go first," she said. "How are *you* feeling?"

He sucked in a deep breath, then let it out in a long huff. "Honestly? I feel like crap, Ellie. I can't sleep, I can't eat. And I don't think any of that's going to change until you come home."

The revelation struck her like a freight train barreling down the track. She'd left without having a heart-to-heart, which she might have owed to him. But there was no way she'd roll over and return to what they'd had.

"I can't go back to the ranch. If I did, then I'd be the one who couldn't sleep or eat." In truth, she wasn't doing much sleeping or eating anyway.

"I'm sorry," he said. "And I hate to admit this, but I really let you down."

At that, her ears perked up. What had he done? Had he talked to the press? Had he managed to sneak around and get the planning commission to approve that blasted hotel he was dead set on building?

"I didn't mean for it to happen," he said.

Her heart battered her rib cage. "Steven, what did you *do*?"

"I didn't keep my promise. I couldn't." He got to his feet, reached into his pocket and pulled out a small black velvet box.

Tears welled in her eyes, and the words wadded up in her throat, making it difficult to breathe, let alone speak.

"I promised you that we'd be friends, that this

would be a marriage in name only. But—" He reached for her hand, and when she placed it in his, he drew her to her feet. "I don't want to just be friends. I don't want to get a divorce. Not now, not ever. I love you, Ellie."

Her heart stalled in her chest, and she tried to wrap her mind around what he was saying. What she hoped he was saying. "Are you sure about that?"

"I struggled with it long enough, but it's the only answer I have for my foul mood, for snapping at anyone who crosses my path. I just hope you're struggling for the same reason."

"I am. I love you, too. I didn't mean for it to happen, but it did. And I was afraid to tell you."

"Don't ever hold back, Ellie. I want to know it all. Be my friend, my lover and my partner in life."

He lifted the velvet lid, revealing a sparkling diamond, and her heart swelled to the point she thought it had filled with helium and would fly out of her chest.

"Will you be my real wife?" he asked.

She could scarcely speak, so she nodded. Somehow, the words seemed to bust their way through the lump in her throat. "Yes, I will."

He removed the ring and slipped it on her finger. "Our engagement might have started out fake, but our wedding was the real deal. And so is my love for you."

As he took her into his arms, she kissed him with all the love in her heart.

When they came up for air, he cupped her face and gazed into her eyes. "Since we're always going to be honest with each other, I have to admit something else. I felt a little hurt that you didn't ask me to go to the doctor with you. I want to be your baby's father in every sense of the word."

"My next appointment is in three weeks," she said. "I'd love to have you go with me. In the meantime… Wait here."

She hurried to the bedroom and went to the nightstand, where she'd left the small scrapbook she'd created after her first visit to the obstetrician and took it to him. "Look at this."

"What is it?" he asked.

"Open it and see."

He did, and a slow smile stretched across his lips as he saw the sonogram images she'd been saving. "This is amazing."

"Meet George Steven Fortune. You'll have to wait until August to see him in person, so these will have to do for now."

"This is awesome," he said. "Little George will be here before we know it. We'll have to get busy so we can turn my guest room into a nursery."

Ellie bit down on her bottom lip. "Would you mind if we lived here? In my house?"

"Don't you like the ranch?"

"I love it. But I'd like some private time while we create our family."

"I'd like that, too. Will Daria mind having a new roommate?"

"Actually, she got a new job and moved out. So it'll just be the two of us. And Tank."

"I'll live anywhere, as long as you're with me. Besides, it's closer to the construction office and several of our job sites. With the wellness spa opening in a week and the restaurant opening in May, I'll be busy. And I won't miss the commute from the ranch."

"What about the hotel?" she asked. "What's going on with that?"

"To tell you the truth, I'm not sure if it'll ever come to fruition, but that's okay. I don't mind putting that project on the back burner for a while. You and I have a baby to get ready for."

"My parents will insist upon helping. I hope you don't mind."

"Not at all. I'm going to like having them as in-laws, especially your mom."

Ellie kissed him again. "You are going to be the best husband ever."

"I thought I already was."

She laughed. "You've got that right."

"That reminds me, I owe you a honeymoon," he said. "Would it be okay if we started it today? Right now?"

"There's nothing I'd like better." Ellie took him by the hand and led him to her bedroom.

As they stood beside her bed, Steven kissed her again—long and deep—savoring the feel of her in his arms, the taste of her on his tongue. He slid his hands along the curve of her back and over the slope of her derriere.

"I love you," she whispered as she removed her green top, revealing a lacy white bra.

A surge of desire shot right through him, and he felt compelled to stake his claim, but they had the rest of the day and all night. And he intended to use every bit of it.

He watched as she peeled her yoga pants over her hips. *Pinch me*, he thought. Ellie was a dream come true—his dream. His wife.

Her gaze never left his as he removed his clothing, baring himself to her in a slow, deliberate fashion.

When they were both naked, she pulled the comforter from the bed, then lay down and opened her arms, silently inviting him to join her. And he gladly did.

She skimmed her nails across his chest, sending a shiver through his veins and a rush of heat through his blood. They continued to stroke, to touch, to taste until he thought they'd both go crazy if they didn't quench the fire the only way he knew how.

Unable to prolong the foreplay any longer, Steven hovered over her and gazed into her passion-filled eyes. "Are you ready?"

"More than ready."

He entered her slowly at first, and her body responded to his, up and down, in and out. As she met each of his thrusts, they came together in a sexual explosion that damned near took his breath away. And as they lay in the sweet afterglow, the reality of their union was staggering as they celebrated their real love, their real marriage and the promise of a very real happy-ever-after.

* * * * *

*Look for the next book in the new
Harlequin Special Edition continuity
The Fortunes of Texas: Rambling Rose
Fortune's Greatest Risk
by USA TODAY Bestselling Author
Marie Ferrarella
On sale April 2020, wherever Harlequin books
and ebooks are sold.*

*And catch up with the previous
Fortunes of Texas titles:*

*Fortune's Fresh Start
by Michelle Major*

*Fortune's Texas Surprise
by USA TODAY Bestselling Author
Stella Bagwell*

Available now!

COMING NEXT MONTH FROM

◆ HARLEQUIN

SPECIAL EDITION

Available March 17, 2020

#2755 FORTUNE'S GREATEST RISK
The Fortunes of Texas: Rambling Rose • by Marie Ferrarella
Contractor Dillon Fortune wasn't always so cautious. But as a teenager, impulse led to an unexpected pregnancy and a daughter he was never allowed to know. Now he guards his heart against all advances. If only free-spirited spa manager Hailey Miller wasn't so hard to resist!

#2756 THE TEXAN TRIES AGAIN
Men of the West • by Stella Bagwell
Taggert O'Brien has had a rough few years, so when he gets an offer for the position of foreman at Three Rivers Ranch, he packs up and leaves Texas behind for Arizona. But he was not prepared for the effect Emily-Ann Broadmore—a barista at the local coffee shop—would have on him or his battered heart. Can he set aside his pain for a chance at lasting love?

#2757 WYOMING SPECIAL DELIVERY
Dawson Family Ranch • by Melissa Senate
Daisy Dawson has just been left at the altar. But it's her roadside delivery, assisted by a mysterious guest at her family's ranch, that changes her life. Harrison McCord believes *he* has a claim to the ranch and is determined to take it—but Daisy and her newborn baby boy have thrown a wrench in his plans for revenge.

#2758 HER MOTHERHOOD WISH
The Parent Portal • by Tara Taylor Quinn
After attorney Cassie Thompson finds her baby's health is at risk, she reluctantly contacts the sperm donor—only to find Woodrow Alexander is easily the kindest, most selfless man she's ever met. He's just a biological component, she keeps telling herself. He's *not* her child's real father or the husband of her dreams...right?

#2759 DATE OF A LIFETIME
The Taylor Triplets • by Lynne Marshall
It was just one date for philanthropist and single mom Eva DeLongpre's charity. And a PR opportunity for Mayor Joe Aguirre's reelection. Giving in to their mutual attraction was just a spontaneous, delicious one-off. But as the election turns ugly, Joe is forced to declare his intentions for Eva. When the votes are counted, she's hoping love wins in a landslide.

#2760 SOUTHERN CHARM & SECOND CHANCES
The Savannah Sisters • by Nancy Robards Thompson
Celebrity chef Liam Wright has come to Savannah to rebrand a local restaurant. And pastry chef Jane Clark couldn't be more appalled! The man who impulsively fired her from her New York City dream job—and turned her life upside down—is now on her turf. And if the restaurant is to succeed, Liam needs Jane's help navigating Savannah's quirky culture...and their feelings for each other.

YOU CAN FIND MORE INFORMATION ON UPCOMING HARLEQUIN TITLES, FREE EXCERPTS AND MORE AT HARLEQUIN.COM.

HSECNM0320

*Harrison McCord was sure he was the rightful owner
of the Dawson Family Ranch. And delivering Daisy
Dawson's baby on the side of the road was a mere
diversion. Still, when Daisy found out his intentions,
instead of pushing him away, she invited him in, figuring
he'd start to see her in a whole new light. But what if
she started seeing him that way, as well?*

*Read on for a sneak preview of the next
book in Melissa Senate's
Dawson Family Ranch miniseries,*
Wyoming Special Delivery.

Daisy went over to the bassinet and lifted out Tony,
cradling him against her. "Of course. There's lots
more video, but another time. The footage of what the
ranch looked like before Noah started rebuilding to the
day I helped put up the grand reopening banner—it's
amazing."

Harrison wasn't sure he wanted to see any of that. No,
he knew he didn't. This was all too much. "Well, I'll be
in touch about that tour."

That's it. Keep it nice and impersonal. "Be in touch"
was a sure distance maker.

She eyed him and lifted her chin. "Oh—I almost
forgot! I have a favor to ask, Harrison."

Gulp. How was he supposed to emotionally distance
himself by doing her a favor?

She smiled that dazzling smile. The one that drew him like nothing else could. "If you're not busy around five o'clock or so, I'd love your help in putting together the rocking cradle my brother Rex ordered for Tony. It arrived yesterday, and I tried to put it together, but it has directions a mile long that I can't make heads or tails of. Don't tell my brother Axel I said this—he's a wizard at GPS, maps and terrain—but give him instructions and he holds the paper upside down."

Ah. This was almost a relief. He'd put together the cradle alone. No chitchat. No old family movies. Just him, a set of instructions and five thousand various pieces of cradle. "I'm actually pretty handy. Sure, I can help you."

"Perfect," she said. "See you at fiveish."

A few minutes later, as he stood on the porch watching her walk back up the path, he had a feeling he was at a serious disadvantage in this deal.

Because the farther away she got, the more he wanted to chase after her and just keep talking. Which sent off serious warning bells. That Harrison might actually more than just like Daisy Dawson already—and it was only day one of the deal.

Don't miss
Wyoming Special Delivery *by Melissa Senate,*
available April 2020 wherever
Harlequin Special Edition books and ebooks are sold.

Harlequin.com